OTHER CZECH LITERATURE IN TRANSLATION
FROM GARRIGUE BOOKS/CATBIRD PRESS

Toward the Radical Center: A Karel Čapek Reader,
edited by Peter Kussi, foreword by Arthur Miller

War with the Newts by Karel Čapek, trans. Ewald Osers

Three Novels by Karel Čapek, trans. M. & R. Weatherall

Catapult by Vladimír Páral, trans. William Harkins

The Four Sonyas by Vladimír Páral, trans.
William Harkins

WHAT
OWNERSHIP'S
ALL ABOUT

by Karel Poláček

Translated from the Czech and
Introduction by Peter Kussi

A Garrigue Book/CATBIRD PRESS

Translation of *Dům na předměstí* (*The House on the Outskirts of the City*),
originally published in 1928, with the kind permission of Jiřina Jelinowicz.

First English-language edition.

CATBIRD PRESS/Garrigue Books
16 Windsor Road, North Haven, CT 06473
Our books are distributed to the trade by
Independent Publishers Group.

Library of Congress Cataloging-in-Publication Data

Poláček, Karel.
[Dům na předměstí. English]
What ownership's all about / by Karel Poláček;
translated from the Czech by Peter Kussi.
p.   cm.
"A Garrigue book."
ISBN 0-945774-19-2 : $19.95
I. Title
PG5038.P64D813   1993
891.8'635--dc20   92-33558 CIP

INTRODUCTION:
A Prisonhouse of Words

The author of *Ownership*, Karel Poláček (pronounced PO-lah-chek), is something of an enigma even in his homeland. If you mention his name to a Czech, the chances are that his face will break into a reminiscent grin: "Oh, Karel Poláček! I loved him when I was a kid! Funny, very funny!" Like most Czechs, he will recall with glee two or three humorous Poláček classics about adolescence, such as the oft-reprinted *There Were Five of Us*. And like most Czechs he will be unaware that this was only a small facet of Poláček's work, and that Poláček was not only a remarkable humorist but also one of the most original Prague writers of the first half of the century, a link between the world of Hašek and Kafka and contemporary authors such as Škvorecký and Hrabal.

Karel Poláček was born in 1892 into a middle-class Jewish family in the small Bohemian town of Rychnov nad Knežňou. His father ran a grocery, and in his youth Poláček helped out in the store. His literary bent and his love of fun and parody were already evident in his high-school years. For example, on the pretense that the Visigoths had been maligned in history as a barbarous and destructive people, he founded a tongue-in-cheek school journal called the *Visigoth Review*, in which he championed the Visigoth cause.

Poláček served on the Russian front in World War I. After the war, Poláček got a job in a commerce agency of the new

Czechoslovak government, a bureaucratic enterprise he described as "an office for official officiating." At the same time, he was writing stories that ultimately came to the attention of the Čapek brothers. These prominent Czech authors were instrumental in obtaining journalistic assignments for Poláček that ultimately gained him a permanent position on the newspaper *Lidové noviny*. Karel Čapek and Poláček became good friends, and indeed they had a lot in common: great respect and affection for the journalistic profession, dislike of clichés and pomposity, a penchant for a down-to-earth, humorous approach to literature. Above all, both Čapek and Poláček placed high value on the apparently commonplace, everyday aspects of life. As Poláček put it: "I avoid sensationalism. The most sensational thing in the world is ordinary life. And in my opinion the highest goal of a writer is to make ordinary life real and fabulous."

Poláček wrote prolifically through the twenties and thirties, in an astonishing variety of genres: novellas, plays, humor books, children's books, sports stories, short stories, as well as newspaper articles and essays. Poláček's major works, in addition to *Ownership*, include a four-volume cycle of novels dealing with the inhabitants of a small Czech town on the eve of the First World War and then during the war itself.

Poláček made no secret of his Jewishness, and Jewish characters and themes appear rather frequently in his work. At the same time, however, he felt himself totally Czech, totally 'assimilated' culturally and linguistically. Unlike Kafka, who wrote only in German, Poláček was an acknowledged virtuoso of the Czech language. After the German invasion of Czechoslovakia in 1939, however, such distinctions became irrelevant; to the Nazis, Poláček was simply a Jew and an anti-fascist intellectual. He was deported to a concentration camp and died in 1944.

Under Nazi occupation, Poláček's work was proscribed. In the postwar communist era, Poláček fared somewhat better; his humorous classics and children's books, in particular, were periodically republished and enjoyed an enthusiastic following. All the same, Poláček's iconoclastic humor, his Jewishness and, above all, his close association with the leaders of the former 'bourgeois' republic did not sit well with the communist government, and his major works were largely ignored. It was therefore little wonder that after so many decades of neglect, Poláček's range and importance have not been fully recognized in his homeland. However, in recent years there has been growing appreciation of Poláček's unique contribution to Czech and European literature, and the 1992 centenary of his birth was marked by an international literary conference in his home town of Rychnov.

Ownership was originally published in 1928, under the title *Dům na předměstí* (*The House on the Outskirts of the City*). In this novel, a policeman builds himself a house on the outskirts of Prague and proceeds to rent out flats to three families. He is polite and subservient at first, but ownership goes to his head and he soon begins to landlord it over his tenants. Step by step, he turns into a tyrant, and the suburban villa turns into a prison for its luckless inhabitants and — ironically — for the tyrannical owner as well.

The landlord-policeman of our novel is a highly original creation. Comical in his strutting self-importance, his sentimentality, and his histrionic rages, he is also a chilling incarnation of the little dictator, a chaplinesque Hitler.

Czech critics at first did not quite know what to make of the novel, though they appreciated its humor and its accurate portrayal of the "small man." Author Marie

Pujmanová declared that Poláček's cop, Jan Faktor, was a unique addition to the characters of world literature. And with the rise of fascism, it became clear that *Ownership* could also be read as a strikingly clairvoyant satire on the genesis of European dictatorship and appeasement.

Some critics were puzzled by Poláček's episodic approach to the novel and, because his subtle use of jargon and cliché both contained and concealed his critique, his vision was not generally recognized. Poláček hated clichés. He wrote: "A liking for empty phrases stems from an ignorance of facts, from thoughtlessness and lack of independent judgment. Clichés can be considered a form of moral bankruptcy."

In 1934, Poláček published *A Journalist's Dictionary*, a collection of hundreds of vapid expressions favored by contemporary journalists. Tomáš Pěkný, an authority on Poláček, points out that throughout the communist era this dictionary was kept under lock and key in closed sections of libraries, testifying to the fact that the passage of time had not diminished its satiric relevance.

Poláček's masterful send-up of everyday speech is fully evident in *Ownership*. The real villains of the suburban villa are not its timid, self-absorbed tenants, not even its pompous tyrannical cop/landlord, but the words that use and mold them: empty, rigid, stereotyped. The bars of their prison-house are made of clichés.

Practically the entire novel consists of reported speech and writing: quoted words, dialogue, statements, notices, legal pronouncements; even people's silent thoughts are conversations with themselves. And yet all the talk is just so much emptiness surrounded by quotation marks.

The characters of *Ownership* make up a broad sample of Czech society of the time; we hear a teacher, a government official, a policeman; we hear the talk of tradesmen, lawyers, landlords, tenants, movers, housepainters; we even hear the voices of departed spirits, the arguments of cats and dogs, the whispers of doors and furniture. They all talk their own language, and yet all these varieties of speech have one thing in common: they are languages of clichés.

If Poláček were not such a gifted humorist, such a connoisseur of the threadbare expression, this jumble of sound could have produced mere monotony and boredom. But like a sculptor working with discarded odds and ends, Poláček slyly manages to transform the trite detritus of speech into a richly meaningful pattern.

Ownership is a very funny novel. It is funny because it is anchored in reality, the realities of language and characterization. The people of the novel are living, believable figures. Its main protagonist, the policeman Jan Faktor, owes his literary existence to one of Poláček's strolls through the city, in the course of which he came upon a house bearing the motto: 'Oh, heart of man, become not the heart of a predator.' Poláček noted: "I was interested in the man who was the author of such a stupid, and yet at the same time such a wise, inscription. I wanted to know the man who could be so lyrically inspired by ownership."

That Poláček correctly deduced the nature of Jan Faktor was proven by an amusing episode: a certain landlord went to see his lawyer, clutching Poláček's novel in his hand. He asked the lawyer to sue Poláček for defamation of character. The lawyer tried to convince his irate client that such a lawsuit would not be successful, whereupon the man exclaimed: "But that's not fair! Why, in this book I absolutely recognize myself!"

PETER KUSSI

Characters and Pronunciation

JINDRICH and **MARIE SYROVY** *Jeend'-rzheek* and *Mah'-ree-ah Sear'-oh-vee* (government clerk and his wife); **Marinka** *Mah'-reen-kah* (nickname for Marie)

JAN and **ANASTAZIE FAKTOR** *Yahn* and *Ahn'-ah-stah'-zee-ah Fahk'-tore* (police sergeant and landlord, and his wife); his house is on **Harant Street** *Hahr'-ahnt*

SAMEC *Sah'-metz* (tailor who is a neighbor of Syrovy's in-laws)

MECL *Maytz'-el* (tailor who lives next door to Faktor's house)

AMINA *Ah'-meen-ah* (Faktor's dog)

MICINKA *Meetz'-een-kah* (Syrovys' cat; the name means 'pussy')

KREJZ *Craze* (news dealer who lives in Faktor's house)

SOLTYS *Shohl'-tees* (teacher who lives in Faktor's house)

GRANDPA HYNEK *He'-nake* (Soltys' dead advisor)

MEJSTRIK *Maced'-rzheek* (neighborhood grocer); **MAJDALENA** *My'-dah-lay-nah* (his wife)

ALOIS *Al'-oh-ees* (Faktor's brother-in-law, the oven man)

UNCLE KRYSTOF *Kree'-shtohf* (Syrovy's greatuncle); also known by his Germanized name **Christoph Otto Kunstmuller**; he lives in **Nove Mesto** *Noh'-vay Me/yehs'-toh* or New City

MRS. MANDAUS *Mahn'-dah/oos* (Faktor's landlady)
Blazenka *Blah'-zhain-kah* (her daughter)
Zpevak *Spee/yehv'-ahk* (Blazenka's fiancé)

SUPITA *Shoo'-pee-tah* (shoemaker who lives across from Faktor's house)

DR. WERICH *Vare'-eek* (notary, lives on **Platner Street** *Plaht'-nairzh*)

This page contain the names and nicknames of the major characters, as well as the pronunciation of their names and of the places they live. If you like to be able to say what you read, this will help a lot. Please note that a / between lettergroups means there is a dipthong, or two vowels that are pronounced separately yet joined together.

This page can be used as a bookmark, for easier reference. Simply cut along the line, or fold the page each way a couple of times and rip the bookmark out.

If this book is yours, don't hesitate to mutilate it, no matter what your teachers said. If it's a library's, please leave the bookmark where it is so that others can use it.

The pronunciations are approximate, as close as possible without lengthy explanation. The order is that of appearance, in most cases.

Chapter One

1   There is a suburb of Prague that lies between two hills. At the top of one hill stands a modern hospital, while at its foot is a cluster of rundown tenements that resemble swallows' nests clinging to the rafters of a farmhouse. And then there is a lone tree, a twisted, bushy pear tree. It is bent with age; nevertheless, in the spring it bursts richly into bloom as a signal that it isn't quite ready to part with life.

The other hill is bare. A short time ago it was covered by patches of wheat waving in the wind. But now the earth is resting, producing only yellowish clumps of wild radish and tall foxtail bleached by the glow of the sun. An abandoned Jewish cemetery spreads out over the summit. It is guarded by an old woman, a half-blind dog, and several hens. The tombstones are sinking into the ground; time has washed away the Hebrew inscriptions, and ivy blankets the departed.

A white road runs through the valley. Noisy trucks are trailed by clouds of dust. By the side of the road there is a small chapel with a holy icon, indicating that this area had once been countryside, which the city government divided into what are known as subdivisions. Not long ago, someone had decorated the Virgin Mary with a wreath of red and blue roses made of crepe paper.

Dappled goats climb the hillocks, nibbling the spiky tips of hawthorn bushes. Ropes carrying brightly colored laundry are strung from pole to pole. A gust of wind puffs up blue undies and ruffles blouses.

Here, the countryside shakes hands with the city. At the borderline stands a wayside cross and the fence of a soccer field. Harantova Street is still part of the city. Its name — Urchin Street — tells us that it is full of dust and soot. A factory making metal instruments blows off smoke in rhythmic intervals: ech — pff — rah!

2   On that street there lived a policeman, and his name was Jan Faktor. He lived in a house that was as unattractive and yellowed as the entire neighborhood, which had been built a few decades earlier by various manufacturing plants to house their workers. The houses are full of cubbyholes, porches, and floppy-shirted children. The air smells of sour gravy and trash.

The policeman was a tall man with broad shoulders, topped by a head as round as a globe. In that head he kept one huge secret which he shared with no one except his wife. She was the sort who tends to be referred to as "that woman." She had thin, tightly clenched lips. And when she did open her mouth, she revealed a set of pale, swollen gums, typical of housekeepers who subsist on bread and coffee. She was thin and agile as a terrified insect scurrying for safety into a crevice. The couple had two children, a retarded boy who sat in front of the door and stared at the street with watery eyes, and a twelve-year-old girl, meager as a wasp and just as agile as her mother.

3   At night, the policeman patrolled the quarter, his helmet gleaming in the light of the lone streetlamp. He'd grab drunkards by their collar and shake them until all rebelliousness was jolted out of them. Thieves he'd handcuff and drag to the station house, where he'd send them flying into a cell with a hefty shove.

The rest of the time he'd pace the dark street with his

14

long stride and ponder his secret thoughts: To play lord and master when you have the wherewithal, that's easy. . . I could do it with my hands tied behind my back . . . But what have I gotten out of life, up to now? Nothing, to be honest . . . But this is idle talk. . . This matter's got to be approached cleverly, otherwise I'll get nowhere. I'll show them all what I'm made of.

During the day he'd sit in the kitchen and help his wife sew neckties and suspenders, which he peddled in offices and apartments. At the end of each week his wife would take their savings to the bank. Some people enjoy throwing money around. But the policeman and his wife reveled in thrift. Their little pile of capital stimulated them and spurred them to ever more intense accumulation. The small, musty kitchen filled with dreams.

Chapter Two

1   One steamy Sunday afternoon, Mr. and Mrs. Syrovy, a government clerk and his spouse, visited the neighborhood. The clerk was in a bad mood because his wife had deprived him of his afternoon nap. He was unable to stop himself from complaining; he grumbled about having to climb the hill. But his wife answered: "I'm taking you up this hill so you'd have a better view of the spot where the house is going to stand." The clerk kept silent, but his annoyance lodged in his parched throat.

A blue sky vaulted overhead. And down below, one

could see a row of two-story houses. Every second one contained a grocery; every third, a tavern. The grocery stores were closed shut by green doors; but out of the taverns came the din of patrons, the clack of billiard balls, and the bang of cardplayers' knuckles against tabletops.

Behind them lay Prague, immersed in a bluish haze. Workers with their families were encamped at the bottom of the hill. The men had taken off their shoes. Floppy-shirted children skipped and shouted. Hot air quivered like calf brains in the window of the butcher store.

"Look," said the wife, pointing at a pile of building material: "down there, those are bricks; they're about to start building." And she pried into the clerk's eyes.

2 But the clerk only sighed, for he'd been overcome by melancholy. He was one of those people who find it difficult to make peace with strange surroundings. He said: "I've never spent any time here. I never heard of any of my friends living in this neighborhood. I am opposed to our moving here. I feel as if I'd never be able to return to the city. And why," he sighed, "is there any need for us to move, anyway? It's better to stay where we are. I'm no friend of novelty."

Whereupon his wife answered: "All right, then. We don't have to move. But I thought you were all for it. If it wasn't for you, I'd never have gone to so much trouble looking for a new place to live. . ."

"But I do want to move," the clerk interrupted her. "I long for the day when we can at last be on our own . . . But why here? The landscape is wild and the people are complete strangers. . ."

"What do you care?" objected his wife. "You don't have to pay attention to anybody. Anyway, we don't have to live here. It's up to you now to find us a more suitable place."

Mrs. Syrovy then proceeded to describe the adventures she had looking for an apartment. Her cheeks burned as she recalled how builders tried to get hold of her dowry, calling it a down payment. She conducted numerous skirmishes with these men, who were motivated by a very simple idea: to build themselves a house using other people's money. She felt angry with her husband for letting her go to battle with men ready to deprive her of her modest dowry, while he sat in his armchair, lazily pondering chess problems. "A proper husband," she added, "would never let his wife run around real-estate offices. He'd take on the job himself."

3   His wife's remarks put the clerk in a dispirited mood. "How peculiar," he mused, "that the acquisition of a dwelling turns out to be such a complicated matter. I know a large number of buildings where people dwell; I know countless people who are owners of spacious and comfortable apartments. Yet my fate commands that my affairs be resolved only with the greatest of obstacles." Aloud, he said: "In general, I would have no objections to your plan. But this place seems somehow peculiar to me. The people here are poor. Odd-looking fellows lounge around with their shoes off . . . The women's faces are all wrapped up in scarves. It's noisy. And the taverns are full of drunkards. Somebody is liable to attack us . . ."

"Don't worry," his wife said firmly, "nobody is going to attack you. We have jails for people like that. As for the drunkards, just step aside and let them go their way."

"But we won't have anyone to associate with. We'll be as lonesome as the first gold-diggers in Arizona. And it's important to have someone to talk with. And the roads are bad. My health is poor. If anything were to happen, you'd never scare up a doctor. I am a government employee and by rights I should be living in a pleasant section like Vinohrady. . ."

"Very well then," Mrs. Syrovy answered sarcastically, "find us a place in Vinohrady. I wouldn't mind living there myself."

The clerk fell silent and his crumpled, freckled face took on the expression of a disgruntled bird. His wife, gloomily taciturn, started walking down the hill, and he quietly followed.

4 When they reached the first row of houses, their attention was aroused by the following scene: a sallow fellow with prominent cheekbones tried to grab a thin woman by the knot of hair on top of her head; she was dressed in a blue blouse, and her face was scratched. Because the sallow fellow was drunk, his hands fumbled in vain for a firm grip on the knot. The woman, bitterly complaining, escaped into the house. The drunk spread his legs wide in order to regain his balance, and muttered: "You filthy swine, I'll kill you even if it means the gallows. It's no use, you slut, I'll get you, my mind is made up. Today. It's all over. You can kneel down and kiss my knees, but my mind is made up. Once I decide to do something, I never back down. Let the whole world see what I'm made of."

Windows flew open and tousled heads gleefully watched the scene. The drunk who could not manage to grasp the knot of hair started to attack other women who had appeared on the battlefield in order to cry shame on him. The drunk, seeing so many female hairdos within reach, tried to grab one. For he was obsessed by the idea that he must knock at least one woman to the ground and drag her by the hair, lest his honor be questioned. The women, however, seethed with fighting spirit. They surrounded the drunk, shrieking like a flock of angry crows. The drunk sank to the ground, his unsteady legs surrendering to the enemy. Then he rose to his feet, his face covered with black mud, only to sink again; and he mumbled that he'll beat them all to a pulp.

On hearing the piercing shrieks, a shoemaker got up from his bench and bravely thrust out his chest, recalling his young days full of quarrels and brawls. He approached the troublemaker with hunched shoulders, assuming the careless slouch typical of professional fighters, who move with a kind of coquettish sloth. Speaking in a mild voice, with words full of friendly advice, he asked the drunk to stop all that silliness and go to bed. He knew perfectly well that this day heaven was about to grant him the pleasure of being able to administer a few good whacks. He could admonish the drunk without any fear that he would be obeyed.

The shoemaker wiped his hands on his leather apron and pleaded: "Look here, Gustaf, listen to me, stop all this nonsense and go to bed. I'm telling you for your own good."

But the drunk stubbornly insisted that he simply had to tear a fistful of hair off some woman's head. And fate ordered him to start in front of the shoemaker's. At that point the shoemaker knew that his hour had struck: he dished out a couple of juicy smacks to both sides of the face. The tormented troublemaker withdrew into the hallway, shouting that the shoemaker would soon get his comeuppance.

The shoemaker wiped his hands on his behind and said with satisfaction: "You've been paid in full. But if it's not enough for you, I'll pay you a dividend as well."

The women continued shouting for a while longer. "It's no wonder he beat up on Ruzena, who is only his cousin, when he mauls his own wife and children day and night!" At that moment the drunk stuck his head out of a second-floor window and yelled: "You just wait, they'll be talking about me all over Prague!"

5 This fracas, which took place right before the eyes of the Syrovys, confirmed the clerk in his conviction that this was a dangerous neighborhood for peace-loving persons. He was terror-stricken, but his anxiety was mixed with a triumphant sense of having been right.

"That's how it goes. . ." he sighed, smiling ruefully. "They want me to put myself at the mercy of murderers. I am supposed to settle down in a place where there's a sinister creature around every corner. No sir! I am neither an armed sheriff called upon to pacify this wild territory, nor a missionary whose mild words engender civilized behavior. I am a clerk in the executive branch and I want to die in peace."

"All right then," his wife said testily, for the brawl had undermined her authority, "I don't insist that this is the only place for us to move to. You're a man, so start taking care of things.

"I've been taking care of everything. Find us a place to live where there are no drunkards, and everything'll be fine. I take care of all the work and you just keep complaining."

The clerk felt anger gurgle in his throat. He took off his bowler and wiped the sweat off his brow. They had to step off the sidewalk to let a group of men dressed in black pass by. Two of them were carrying a wreath with a red and white ribbon. Behind them walked a man with a ribbon across his chest, inscribed "Literary and Educational Society".

"High time for us to get out of here," thought the clerk; "another funeral coming up . . . I'm sure the fellow was beaten to death by some drunkards. And a policeman is nowhere in sight. There is no provision for public safety around here. And this is where they want me to live? Oh no, my dear little woman, I won't let anyone do me in. I'm not as stupid as you may think."

Chapter Three

1   When they returned home, the clerk's father-in-law was sitting in the kitchen on the maid's bed, his feet nestled in a pair of felt slippers with a checkerboard design. He was smoking his meerschaum and cogitating. Dusk was falling and darkness was gathering in the corners of the kitchen. Evening bells resounded over Prague and Father blew gray smoke-rings in the air, pouting like a Christmas carp.

Dusk has the power to awaken thoughts of the past. Father mused about the days when he'd worked as weighmaster at a sugar refinery: It is a freezing morning and stars sparkle in the snow. A fist pounds on the window and a voice says, "Time to get up, weighmaster, sir." One had to get out of bed, like it or not. And those terrible frosts of the old days! What a horror . . . Now he's sitting here all tied up with rheumatism. "Oh my, oh my! How much longer am I going to be around?" The old man nods his head mournfully. "Can those young people be trusted to put up a dignified tombstone for me? I'd like to have it decorated with a photograph on porcelain. . ."

When he caught sight of his son-in-law, he felt like complaining about last night's pressure in his chest.

"I know there are special drops," he began, "which are good against pounding of the heart. But I don't know what they're called. Jindrich, do me a favor and ask the people in your office. . ."

He also felt like launching into a conversation about the peculiar taste in his mouth. But the son-in-law, who wasn't listening, went to his room.

2   In the meantime, Mother-in-law was in the living room, dozing over her newspaper. She sat in an armchair, propped up by pillows; on her short nose, shaped like a knot in wood, rested a pince-nez attached to a ribbon. The sound of footsteps woke her. "Lord, you gave me a fright," she said on seeing the young people. "I just dreamt that we ran out of milk." Sighing, she struggled to her feet; her body was a shapeless dome supported by legs that resembled clay jugs.

The clerk was resting on a couch, pondering his life. "My life is horrible," he mumbled, "and there's no hope of any change. Snips of paper roll around in the corners. Eggshells crunch underfoot. The chairs are decked with underwear and aprons. An eternal draft whistles through the room. My God! Even if I begged her on my knees, she still wouldn't close the doors!"

The wife stepped into the room and as usual began to shift objects back and forth.

"What are you doing?" the clerk asked caustically.

"I am straightening up the room," answered his wife.

"She's always straightening up. She spends a lifetime

straightening up. I can't find a bit of peace anywhere. My head aches, but she doesn't care. . ."

The clerk fixed a hateful glance at the damp rag in his wife's hand. He sees her as his enemy: "Everybody oppresses me," he cogitated gloomily, "and she most of all. What awful material she chose for my suit!"

Indeed, his wife had bought cloth of such a peculiar pattern that the clerk could not escape notice. When he entered the office in his new suit, one of his co-workers rose to his feet, closed his eyes, and put on a bemused expression:

"I don't quite know what category to put you in," he said.

"Where in the world did you find such material?" asked the office messenger. "Very peculiar. I'd say it's the color of bird-seed."

The entire staff of the department gathered round the clerk. They began to turn him this way and that.

"I've got it," said one of his older colleagues. "You remind me of a trout. A trout's back has the same kind of dots. It sure is a strange design. You'll get plenty of attention."

That frightened the clerk, for the one thing he feared most of all was to become an object of attention. He felt as if the light in the office was too bright, and he hunched down behind his desk.

That day he came home angry and declared that he would skip dinner.

"Don't eat, then," his wife said drily, for she guessed what it was about, "but that material is inexpensive and durable. We don't have to impress anyone. People should mind their own business."

The clerk humbled himself and silently ate his soup.

3   They turned on the lights and prepared for supper. The living room was big as a riding stable. The builder who had built the house many years ago was a person who liked quick decisions. He ruled out a square and presto: a room. When he designed adjoining rooms, he found that there wasn't enough space and so he made an alcove. He was like an unskilled seamstress baffled by her material. There is too much for the sleeves, so she makes folds; and then there's not enough. This room grew at the expense of others; in the rest of the apartment one had to crouch down. In the middle of the ceiling there was a star-shaped spot, caused by weather and a leaky roof. One stormy evening water actually dripped into the room. Father would keep his gaze fixed on that star while smoking his pipe. His wife contemplated the star when she tried to decide what to cook tomorrow.

This evening, Father puffed gloomily on his pipe until his thin temples bubbled up like the forehead of a horse chomping on a bag of oats. He was getting ready to say something when the doorbell rang. A neighbor came to borrow the key to the attic. But this turned out to be a mere pretext. The woman came to announce that early in the morning a plainclothes detective had come to the house and arrested a gang of thieves who had been traveling through the area robbing stores.

"Just imagine!" Mother exclaimed in amazement. "And we knew nothing about it!"

The clerk felt his heart stop beating.

"Thieves!" he thought, terror-stricken. "How awful! I've fallen into the clutches of robbers!" he moaned. "It's a wonder I escaped annihilation."

A lively debate about evil people ensued. Father contributed his theory that the safest house is one occupied by thieves. He said: "We can live peacefully, because we're guarded by thieves."

"That's true," the neighbor agreed, "but just the idea of it!"

Father maintained that he had long suspected something fishy going on.

He said: "I've noticed what those young fellows living in the little room next to us bring home for supper: Edam cheese, Portuguese sardines, and Hungarian salami. That sort of thing means an early visit from the police. It's already the third such case . . . When thieves succeed in a job they always feast on delicacies." The neighbor left, satisfied that she had managed to bring such an interesting piece of news.

Father grew pensive, wanting to contribute several thoughts about the deterioration of safety and the disorder in the building. He was about to launch into a lecture about the need for carefully locking all doors and paying careful attention to any stranger seen on the stairs. But his son-in-law was irritated by the old man's face, with its folds resembling an accordion. He looked with contempt upon his father-in-law's waxed mustache, which stuck out like bristles above the petrified mouth. And he was especially incensed by the round head with its narrow brow, behind which dwelled haughtiness, stubbornness, and quarrel-someness. In order to avoid a conversation, he quickly finished his supper and left. His wife followed him to their room.

4   There he said: "Come what may — I don't intend to spend the rest of my life under that star on the ceiling. I don't want to listen to your mother's complaints about the high cost of food. I don't want to be the victim of your father's lectures. I, too, feel like living. Do I have to keep looking at underwear draped over the furniture, at pots of stewed fruit looming over the cupboards like parapets? Am I to be forever pursued by the pot of lard standing on the piano right next to the majolica vase where Father stores his pipe-tobacco? Must I forever watch the doors opening by themselves, as if signaling the passage of long-departed fathers-in-law whose souls have not been granted eternal rest because in this life they hadn't fully explicated their views regarding thieves?"

"Speaking of thieves," answered his wife, who was determined to strike while the iron was hot, "what kind of city is this? What kind of safety do we have? How can a decent family live in a house containing a robbers' nest? I want to live in my own place. I want my kitchen to shine with white cleanliness. My mind boggles when I see how sloppily they handle kitchen equipment in this place. But what can be done? You refused to move because you're terrified of quarrelsome neighbors."

"I think you misunderstood me," answered the clerk. "I only expressed my dislike of drunkenness. I believe that brawls and drunkenness thrive among the people, but that in other ways the common folk are mild-mannered and sincere. I long to be delivered from this den of thieves. I want to move away and I hope that you will submit to my wishes without resistance."

"I always do what you want," his wife answered. "You've decided to move and that's that. Only don't blame me later. I have asked our future landlord to visit us, because we must work out a lease."

"Let him come. I'll give him a proper welcome."

Chapter Four

1   One day the bell rang and there at the door was a policeman in uniform. He was followed by a tall, bony woman with a smooth hairdo and a bun in the form of a figure eight. The policeman asked whether Mr. Syrovy was at home.

"My God!" exclaimed the clerk's mother-in-law, frightened. "What's the matter?"

"I have something to discuss with him."

"Come in. He's home," she said. The uniformed policeman made her worried. "Jindrich," she called into the room, "you have visitors."

"I am Sergeant Faktor and this is my wife," the policeman introduced himself.

"Welcome, welcome," said the clerk, rubbing his hands. "Marie, come here, we have guests."

The brawny policeman grasped the clerk's hand and gave it a hefty shake. It would be hard to imagine a more mismatched pair: the clerk stood next to the sergeant like a sparrow beside a rooster, and tried to puff up his insignificant chest.

The clerk's wife came in, and the policeman greeted her with a blustery "pleased-to-meet-you-madam;" the bony woman piped up the same greeting. The policeman sat down in the chair offered him, and his wife folded herself like a carpenter's yardstick into a nearby armchair.

The door, having guessed that Mother was anxious to overhear what was going on, opened wide.

2   The policeman turned out to be an exceptionally talkative person who liked to use choice language.

He began: "Well then . . . if, as they say, we reach an agreement, I will be your landlord and you will be my tenants."

"That is so," the clerk agreed.

"I am exactly the man," the policeman continued, "you see before you. I don't like unnecessary words and beating about the bush. My only desire is to get along with people. You can ask anybody you like and they will tell you: Sergeant Faktor is a man who minds his own business and keeps his nose out of other people's affairs. With these hands," and he stretched out his hairy hands, "I have labored all my life and I have always been thrifty. Now I've gotten a parcel of land from the city on which I will build my house. I can tell you that I don't waste time even when off duty, because my wife and I sew neckties which we sell from door to door. I don't waste a single minute, because I want to achieve something in life."

"That's the way to do it," said the clerk.

"You can believe me when I tell you that this business has cost me a lot of running around and hard thinking. Now I am more or less ready; I have it all worked out in my head. There is only one thing missing: some decent people as tenants."

The clerk straightened his back and squared his shoulders.

"Look here, I'll tell it to you straight. Next door to me, a certain tailor named Mecl is about to build a house. He boasted to me that a doctor is going to move in. I thought to myself: you piddling needle-pusher, are you trying to show off? I want to give him this answer: My future tenant is a government official. Take that!"

"I wish," squeaked the policeman's wife, "that our

house would have the inscription: 'Built with our callouses.' " And then at once she fell silent and clenched her thin lips into a hyphen.

"Be quiet," the policeman brushed her aside. "There will be an inscription, but a different one. I have already taken care of that. I think of everything."

"And what about. . ." the clerk remarked shyly, "as far as . . . in other words . . . the actual terms?" Mr. Syrovy was rather abashed to talk about the commercial side of things after the policeman had shown so much feeling and idealistic enthusiasm.

"Terms?" the policeman exclaimed with a smile. "There need be no terms between us. Dear sir, you don't know me. I am exactly the kind of person. . . Well! I just took one look at you and I saw that the two of us will never go separate ways. I meet everybody more than halfway, providing they show good will. You needn't concern yourself about terms. We'll just have a lawyer draw up a contract and we'll put in everything you wish. I'll do everything possible to accommodate you."

3   They set out for the office of the lawyer, who lived a few doors down on the same street. He and the clerk had been schoolmates, and he had only recently opened his law office. The lawyer intended to use this occasion for showing off before his former classmate. In the manner of the lawyers of old, he meant to use a silent gesture to motion the two parties to their seats, which were typical lawyers' chairs with the kind of shabby covers that suggest dignity. He meant to hear out their case with a slightly frowning forehead and to indicate mild impatience by toying with his watch-chain. He meant to lean back in his armchair, join his extended fingertips in a bored gesture, and begin his discourse in a dry, legal voice free of any hint of passion.

Instead, he became muddled and began to grimace and laugh needlessly. Then he stopped, for it occurred to him: "What in the world am I doing? I don't follow my own plan: I was going to have my secretary tell them: 'Sir Lawyer is occupied and asks both parties to wait.' " He tried to think of a way to reclaim his dignity, and abruptly launched into an explanation of §1091 through §1121 of the Civil Code. He maintained that §1096 states that "the lessor is duty-bound not to hinder the usage of the object which is the subject of the rental agreement." On the other hand, §1098 states that "tenants and leaseholders are entitled to use objects rented or leased for a definite period, and also to sublet them, providing such activity does not harm the property of the owner and providing it is not expressly forbidden in the contract. . ."

The clerk listened to this harangue in quiet, tired dejection, and thought: "What is he trying to say? What paragraphs is he talking about? He is trying to put on airs for no reason. Why is he wearing sideburns and leather spats? There was no need for us to come here, of all places."

The policeman spoke up: "Well, Counselor . . . the law is full of paragraphs, that's for sure. But Mr. Syrovy and I will come to an agreement, and I trust that we'll never end up in court, we'll stay loyal to one another." And he placed his paw on the clerk's shoulder.

The gentleman with the sideburns coughed drily and said: "I only wanted to acquaint you with the legal aspects of a rental agreement. Now we can get to the heart of the matter."

He pressed the bell and after a while a typist appeared,

carrying sheaves of paper; her face was swathed in a bandage.

The lawyer glanced at her gloomily and thought: "Why does she have to look like that today, of all days. It's enough to make one mad. What decent lawyer employs a typist that looks like an Egyptian mummy?" Aloud, he said: "Are you ready, Miss? All right then, please write: The contract, concluded this day — eh — between. . ." Stroking his chin, he strode back and forth with long strides.

4   They concluded a contract: The party of the first part rents etc. etc. in a house to be built on lot no. so and so, an apartment including the use of garden etc., for a period of four years; in return for which, the party of the second part is to furnish four years' rent, in advance. The lawyer rose to his feet and shook the hands of both parties with the fatherly expression of a doctor dismissing a successfully treated patient.

The participants shook off the depressing feeling that accompanies any official proceeding, and a lively conversation ensued.

The policeman heaved a sigh of satisfaction: "Well, that's over and done with."

"I'm glad it's over, too," said the clerk.

"One thing worries me," said Mrs. Syrovy. "Will there be enough room for hanging the wash?"

"You bet!" exclaimed the policeman. "There'll be lots of space!"

"I intend to grow dahlias," said the clerk.

"But don't forget vegetables," the policeman commented; "it's a real advantage to have one's own celery, carrots, and cabbage. You save a lot of money that way."

"Certainly. But cultivating dahlias gives you all kinds of

pleasure. You plant them and you wait, all excited, to see what's going to pop out. It's quite amusing when the colors come out totally different from what you expected."

"Then again," the policeman countered indulgently, "we mustn't let a bunch of dahlias stand in the way of cabbage, which goes so well with meat."

"We'll feed the cabbage stalks to our rabbits," mused Mrs. Faktor.

"Oh yes, rabbits!" the clerk burst out enthusiastically. "What marvelous animals! Their fur is like silk!"

"Well, the fur isn't worth a whole lot," the policeman remarked. "But if you're talking about rabbit in sour cream sauce, I'm your man."

"Can we raise poultry?" asked Mrs. Syrovy.

"Poultry will fill the yard with a merry hubbub," the clerk said, "and the cock will greet the dawn with his mighty crowing."

"I have no objection," the policeman replied, "though you've got to make sure the birds don't tear up the garden."

"And what about a peacock?"

"Peacocks are unprofitable."

"But what a beautiful bird! He'll reign over the throngs of ordinary poultry; he'll wear a crown of opalescent blue; and perched on the garden wall, he'll display the gorgeous fan of his tail."

"Peacocks don't bring in any profit," repeated the policeman, "and they create an unnecessary mess. But if you really want a peacock, so be it. I won't stand in your way. I'll agree to everything."

"My spouse loves roses. Do you intend to decorate the walls of your house with climbing roses?"

"I've considered that, too. Anything you can think of, you'll have. You'll live with us like it was heaven."

Chatting this way, they reached the streetcar stop. There they parted, with prolonged hand-shaking all around. The policeman kept saying: "Well, I sure am pleased," and the clerk repeated: "I'm pleased, too."

Chapter Five

1   Under the star on the ceiling, chilly dampness wafts through the room. Felt slippers with a checkerboard design shuffle around the kitchen and mumble phrases about children's lack of respect.

Mother-in-law sighs: "That's how it is."

Father-in-law: "There's an old proverb: Ingratitude rules the world."

Mother: "They're so secretive."

Father: "She's worse than he is."

"You don't have to tell me. I've been watching her for a long time."

"Oh yes."

"That's how it is."

Father draws a pipe cleaner through his pipe. Then he goes to wind up the grandfather clock. "The devil knows," he grumbles, "why you people keep fiddling with that clock. If you don't know what you're doing, leave it alone. That's what I'm here for. Sure . . . Everything around here is about to go to pieces."

"They ought to realize how awful they are," Mother says gloomily, grating a piece of gingerbread. "If they want to move out, let them. Nobody's standing in their way. But why didn't they have the decency to come to me and say: 'Mom, we're looking for a new place to live?' Don't we deserve at least that much respect?"

"We sure mean a whole lot to them," Father said with bitter irony.

"Did they have such a bad life with us?" Mother exclaimed pathetically. "Didn't I cook pork chops for that nearsighted stinker, just because he doesn't like beef with tomato sauce?"

"It's your fault for spoiling him," Father said severely. "You don't like it — don't eat it!"

"And she goes off and buys herself a new hat and doesn't have the common decency to come and show it to me. Oh, the good Lord will punish you for your treachery! What have I done to deserve such a mean child?" complained Mother.

"Be quiet," Father says.

"Why should I be quiet? A proper daughter would come and say: Mom, I have a new hat, how do you like it?"

"I'm telling you to be quiet. I don't want to hear any more of your talk."

"Are you giving me orders? Just look at yourself. The whole day you loaf around in your slippers. Go do something useful. I'm sick of you."

Father flared up like a pile of resinous wood.

"Woman!" he shouted. "How dare you! How dare you insult a sick person! Don't fool around with me, I have a weak heart. If you had a drop of kindness, you'd have some sympathy for my eye troubles. I can't even read anymore, I'm so dizzy. That's what I get for all my benevolence, for having sacrificed myself. . ."

"I haven't noticed any benevolence. And where are the sacrifices?"

34

"She's killing me," Father gasped; "she's tormenting me to death. She wants to send me to my grave. Just remember how you insulted me! Oh, you'll have pangs of conscience on your deathbed!"

"So be it," he added with scorn, putting on his shoes, "I'm leaving forever. You'll never see me again. I am going away . . . I'll find myself a small room somewhere and finish the rest of my days there."

"Good. I'll have some rest at last," said his wife.

"Yes, you're right," Father mumbled, savoring his humiliation, "everything is just fine, I know . . . You don't need me anymore. I'm no good for anything. You can chase me from your door. I'm going; I won't stand in your way. . ."

"She really fixed me good," he muttered under his breath on his way out. "Such a woman! To think I could have had a bride pretty as a flower, the daughter of a liquor distributor. Graceful, rich, kind, decent . . . Was I out of my mind? I must have been out of my senses to marry this old bag. . ."

The door closed with a thunderous bang. The decrepit house shook. Curious heads poked out of holes and crannies. Mother ran into the hallway and shouted, leaning over the railing: "You couldn't even come to our house until Anna put a pair of soles on your tattered old shoes! So there!" And she shut the door behind her.

2   Father hunkered down on the stairs, a sorry knot of woe. He moaned: "Friends! Good people! Look at me! My own wife chased me out of the house . . . I'm a homeless old man . . . Oh Lord! She wanted to kill me, have mercy on me. . ."

The tailor Samec ran out, a tape measure draped over his shoulders.

"What's the matter, neighbor?" he said sympathetically, lifting the old man up. "You mustn't take it to heart. Everything will turn out for the best. Come on in, we'll give you a cup of coffee. Everybody has his troubles. . ."

Father got up with difficulty and said in a weary voice: "Thank you, Mr. Samec. I know that you mean well. But I am beyond help. My last hour has struck. She," he whispered secretively, looking over his shoulder, "she wants to poison me . . . I know all about it . . . There they go, you see them? They got together with her to kill me off. . ."

The clerk and his wife were coming up the stairs.

"Go and look to your handiwork," Father said to his spouse in a broken voice. Then he got up and left.

"Where is he going?" the clerk asked, worried.

"To the café," his wife answered drily.

"But what . . . what handiwork is he talking about?"

"They must have quarreled, that's all. You know what they're like."

Ill humor seeped through all the corners of the house.

"Pi - ty, pi - ty, pi - ty," intoned the clock. Mother did not respond to the young couple's greeting. A pile of dirty dishes shifted in the sink with a dry clatter. Gloomy mustiness wallowed through the air. The rusty cat, hunched by the door, was getting ready to slip out, for she loved quiet, peaceful well-being and hated domestic quarrels.

"Get out!" Mother stamped her foot when she noticed the clerk and his wife. "I don't want to see you! You're the cause of all my misfortunes! High time I got rid of you!"

The couple stopped in the doorway and turned on their heels.

"Let's go to the movies," the wife decided.

3   A balmy evening murmurs through the streets. Streams of people collide at corners. A brightly lit advertisement announces that "Maud opened the letter and her bosom heaved with emotion. Read the conclusion of this torrid novel." An enormous Osram light bulb blinks and then glows red, then blinks again and surrounds itself with a pale-blue halo. Women, sensing men at their back, stop in front of store windows. An old woman stands in front of a pastry shop, nods and rustles like aspen leaves in an autumn breeze: "Bless you, gentlemen, bless you, gentlemen!" A man with a green scarf is standing next to a table on which a sleepy sparrow-hawk is mulling things over, and he shouts: "Top prize one hundred thousand, last chance, drawing tomorrow!"

The Syrovys keep on walking.

The wife smiles, deep in her own thoughts.

"He told us," she says, "that we can move in the fall. Everything is supposed to be ready by the first of October."

"Autumn will be here before we know it," the clerk replied.

"We can be glad that our landlord is a policeman. He won't cheat us."

"He's got to keep his pension in mind. And he'll protect us from criminals."

"How thoughtful and deliberate he is!"

"I like him too. We'll be able to live in permanent friendship."

"And she," the wife said, suppressing a flutter of vanity, "she called me Madam!"

"That's wrong," the clerk said vehemently; "I won't stand for such kowtowing. I want to be an equal among equals. I'll try to make them forget that we belong among the better class of people. I want to fraternize with the common folk. . ."

He pondered for a while and then said: "And in my spare time I'll devote myself to gardening. I'll get some expert literature and study it diligently. Oh, how I look forward to that! I'll dig and hoe; my muscles will harden and my visage will bloom with a copper hue!"

And he straightened himself up, as if he already felt fresh sap flowing in his veins.

His wife thought: "It's a good idea for him to work in the garden. We won't have to hire a gardener. And we'll save on vegetables."

4   When they returned home, Father had already gone to bed. He was smoking. His round head was encased in a black night-cap. A curl of gray hair stuck out from under the down comforter on the other bed.

"I am telling you . . . puff - puff - puff . . . that I know the exact moment when this sickness first came over me," Father said, narrating some old story from his life.

"Is that so?" said his wife.

"I was . . . puff - puff - puff . . . just a boy of thirteen. I was standing by the fence and suddenly I felt a poisonous wind blowing on me. And that did it. From that time on I haven't been the same . . . I can barely move. . ."

"I'm buying myself a special ointment," said the gray curl. "Hedda gave me a prescription."

The clerk and his wife poked in their heads, wished the old folks good night, and went to their room.

"He didn't even ask me how I was feeling," complained Father.

"Don't bother with him. He's worse than she is. She was always respectful to us."

The clerk said, undressing: "You know how I'll fix up the flower-beds? In the first row, I'll plant crocuses, in the second row miniature hyacinths, and tulips in between."

He slipped under the cool comforter. "Or else," he continued, "I'll put blue hyacinths or squill up front, with pink hyacinths in back. . ."

"And what about carrots, cabbage, celery?" his wife interrupted.

"Be patient, everything will be taken care of . . . I also want to cultivate monk's-hood. But careful! It's poisonous."

His wife lay down and put out the light.

"And don't forget the perennials! Just wait till you see the perennials!"

"Leave me alone, I feel awfully tired today."

"Perennials, perennials," the clerk mumbled as he embraced his wife.

"Perennials," he heaved a deep sigh as he climbed back into his own bed.

"You know, I was the only one in the whole class who knew that the scientific name for ladyslippers was *cypripedium calceolus*. . ."

Then he fell asleep.

Chapter Six

1   The suburban hill comes to life with the bustle of construction. Men bare to the waist are standing in excavated pits, tossing up arching shovelfuls of dirt. A woman with a kerchief on her head mixes smoking lime in a barrow. Loads of bricks rattle on carts; drivers, their legs swathed military fashion in strips of cloth, fill the air with shouts at their horses. Piles of sand have attracted the attention of floppy-shirted youngsters. A shaggy, black little dog, his tail curled up like a watchspring, scurries among the workers. The dog enjoys the hubbub and commotion. He has no master, because everyone orders him about. Nobody knows how he landed on the building site. Perhaps he was hired with the others, as a helper. Up till then he'd been dragging himself through the countryside, homeless, experiencing the callousness of villagers. But now he has been given the job of watchman, and the dog is proud to be liberated from vagrancy and given a firm place in the social order. And he is determined to be kind and attentive toward the workers, but tough and unyielding toward anyone without that special construction odor about him. At night, when the construction site is deserted, the black dog paces around the hut containing tools and equipment. With every suspicious noise, he braces himself on his front legs, pricks up his ears, and emits a brusque, angry bark. The dog certainly overdoes his watchkeeping fervor; he is anxious for the praise of his superiors.

The policeman stands in the midst of the workers,

swinging a pickax. Bits of earth, which have hardened from resting too long, spray all around. He is wearing frayed burlap trousers; on his head he sports an old police cap, the torn crown of which is surrounded by a rusty wire; an open shirt reveals his hairy chest; and the muscles on his back move like transmission belts. His every motion, calculated and precise, betrays his peasant origin.

2 In the city, bells began to ring and the tower clock struck high noon. The policeman stuck his shovel in the ground. Workers start to crawl out of their holes. They untie colorful kerchiefs containing a hunk of bread with a dab of butter on the side. The policeman's wife has brought him a pot of soup in a waxed-cloth bag. He ate his soup quickly, standing up, like a soldier on the march. He kept one eye on the pot, the other on the completed work. As soon as he finished eating he again picked up his tool. His wife collected the dishes and left, followed by the black dog, whose pitiful whimpering meant: "What about me? I get nothing?"

The policeman shaded his eyes; he recognized the clerk scrambling toward him over piles of building materials.

"Ah, we have a visitor!" A big smile broadened his face.

"Yes, yes." The clerk shifted his feet and glanced around. He felt like saying something jovial, but nothing occurred to him.

"I see the work has started," he blurted out after a while; he was ashamed at once of his foolish remark.

"You bet. We're building, building. It's criminally hard work."

The workers began to nudge one another.

"That dry bread is hard to swallow," said a fellow with a prominent adam's apple.

"Something's needed to wash it down," a young man with a cleanshaven neck chimed in.

"That's for sure. You look like your throat's gone dry."

"That's right. And you seem about ready for a pint. . ."

"You bet. A bit of cold beer would hit the spot."

"Beer gives a man strength."

The clerk understood at last. He pulled out a twenty-crown coin and said, blushing: "Here you are, gentlemen. Have a beer on me."

"Now, now," the worker with the adam's apple remonstrated, "there was no need for that. We just like to horse around a bit, just for fun." But he took the money and shouted: "Frank, off with you. Cold beer. And make it snappy." The younger worker wiped his hands on his pants and scurried off. The clerk became the center of attention. He didn't know what to say and shifted from one foot to the other, smiling guiltily. Then he said goodbye and quickly departed.

He heard someone calling after him. He turned around and saw a group of workers with arms around each other's shoulders, saluting him with uplifted glasses of beer. The clerk stopped and waved back.

An old man with a pale, swollen face sat on the doorstep of one of the houses; a pair of crutches was lying next to him.

The man said, breathing heavily: "Sir, it's not a good idea to give them beer money."

"Why?" asked the clerk.

"Well . . . you shouldn't encourage them . . . they start drinking and then they fool around instead of working. Lazy bastards!" And the old man spat in a long arc. "Nobody supports me, either," he said enviously; "they tell me: How come you're taking it easy? I am not taking it easy, I'm a cripple. If I had the strength, I'd be glad to work."

The clerk reached in his wallet and gave the old man a crown.

"God bless you!" the oldster screeched after him.

3   After lunch the workers crawled out of their holes; bricklayers started piling bricks; walls sprouted upward; and then they built a scaffold around them. The policeman stood on the top and gave orders like a captain from his bridge. If there was a bit of bricklaying to be done, he did it; but he also knew his way around carpentry and other construction trades, for when he used to patrol the streets as part of his police duties, he would stop and watch the hands of the workers. And he learned a lot, for a policeman is supposed to keep his eyes open, especially if he wants to become a landlord.

While busily at work, he speculated how to increase his property and turn everything to profit.

"I won't let the tenants use the attic," he decided. "They can hang their laundry in the yard. The attic will be used for breeding pigeons."

He became lost in thought; in his mind he already saw pigeons high in the sky, flying in perfect circles. Unawares, he stuck out his palm and lured invisible pigeons with an inaudible whistle.

He stopped his musing and gazed suspiciously at the site of his neighbor, the tailor Mecl, who was building a house for a daughter that was due to get married in the spring. When the neighbor's house was progressing faster than his own, the policeman impatiently prodded his workmen to hurry; and he was pleased to see that he had overtaken the tailor.

All the same, the work was progressing slowly, for the

policeman lacked sufficient funds and had to let several workers go. After that he had to build alone with only the help of his father and brother-in-law, a tall, gloomy man with eyes that kept tearing as if he suffered from an eternal cold.

The policeman ruled despotically over the two of them, and they obeyed without resistance. The policeman urged them on to ceaseless haste. He even grumbled at the evening shadows that enveloped the unfinished work, and he felt like stopping time and pushing back the night. The policeman's father was hoping that his son would give him shelter in his old age, and the policeman also promised his gloomy in-law that he would lend him money for fixing up a workshop.

Chapter Seven

1   The summer fled, and autumn arrived. A violent wind burst into the neighborhood and ripped hats off people's heads. It whistled, moaned, and created havoc. Goats climbed the hill and pensively chewed their cud. Geese collected in flocks and suddenly, as if they had agreed on a signal, spread their wings with a penetrating shriek and ran down the street, swaying from their waist like peasant-women. The wind swelled the laundry hanging in a lot surrounded by a fence; it puffed up chemises and blouses and climbed into men's shorts, blowing them up like a bladder. Fluttering on the electric wires overhead were pieces of colorful paper, torn off the tails of kites. The policeman succeeded in covering the roof before the onset of winter. Then he quarreled with his father, who left for his village convinced that nowadays a parent never gets a smidgeon of gratitude from his children. When the policeman's brother-in-law asked, "so where's the money you promised," the policeman answered; "we'll just have to wait and see how we're making out." His brother-in-law looked at him through his teary eyes, reached into a fold of his cap with his bony, lime-spotted hand, pulled out a cigarette butt, gloomily lit it, and left.

2   "It's like this," the policeman explained to the clerk, who had come to look at the construction: "I wanted everything to be ready by fall, but I miscalculated. My people all disappeared, and Dad got some bug in his head and left. He was stubborn. I told him: you want to be stubborn? So can I. Are you angry? So am I. He can't forgive me for taking a wife against his will. He said: You'll marry Marie. Me: I don't want your Marie. I have my own. He: Just cast your eye at Marie's bosom and hips and you'll see I'm right; she'd be just right for you. As for that woman of yours, why, she looks like a starved wasp. Shake up your brain and think. Me: You're not marrying her, I am. And once I make up my mind, I don't back down. That's me."

The policeman pulled out a tape and started to measure the windows. After a while he stopped, straightened up, and pushed his cap back on his head. Then he continued:

"And my old lady, you know her, if she says anything bad about me, don't listen to her. That bag could eat you out of house and home. If there's a juicy morsel in the house I've got to lock it up, otherwise it's gone. I could tell you tales! You know, I make stuffed animals for children.

Once I was making an elephant out of velour. The tusks, covered with white cotton mesh, were finished and lying on the table. The old bag walks around the table and stares at the tusks. I thought: what the hell is that bag looking at? As soon as I turn my back, she grabs one of the tusks and sticks it in her craw. When she realized that I was looking at her, she quickly put the tusk back and mumbled: 'How silly of me! Here I thought it was a cream-filled horn!' Ha, ha! I'll give you a cream-filled horn, you ravenous old bag!"

He reached down, picked up a can of paint, and carried it out into the hallway.

"And as for my brother-in-law. . . Just look how thin he is. He's eaten up by avarice. His eyes are too big. Whatever he sees, he's got to have. He's always sucking up to me with his 'give me this, lend me that.' I'll give nothing, I'll lend nothing. Nobody gives me anything, either. I used to be stupid, but no more."

The clerk listened and listlessly scraped the white-washed wall with his fingernail. He thought: that's all well and good, but what does it have to do with me? Aloud, he said: "Yes, some people. . ."

"Save your money, I said to my in-law, save like I do, and you'll have money, too. I don't ask nothing from anybody. He took it as an insult and left. All right, go with my blessing. But now you see why I couldn't finish the house. You see the troubles I have. . ."

3 There was no helping it, the clerk had to spend the winter in the old house. And winter was rapidly coming on, and the old house sank into ever deeper gloom. Snowflakes streamed horizontally through the streets; gusty winds played plaintive melodies on the drainpipes and moaned in the chimneys. On the street the snow turned into a black paste that stuck to the trousers of pedestrians. The star on the ceiling oozed like an old wound. Doors opened on their own, windows rattled nervously.

Yet the clerk no longer saw the depressing darkness, he ignored the star on the ceiling. He already lived in his future garden; he saw himself leaning over the flowerbeds. When he did glance at the star on the ceiling, it turned into a beautiful flower of a remarkable color. "This flower," his lips whispered sweetly, "has been cultivated in my garden. It is called Dahlia Maxima Syrovy. It derives from a genus of wild dahlias. Throngs of botanists travel from afar to see this wonder. They must hurry. For the Dahlia Maxima Syrovy blooms but once in a human lifetime."

Even the yellow building next to the produce market was bathed in honeycolored light. The government office where the clerk worked, separated by glass partitions from the noisy throng of law clerks, attorneys, secretaries, and various predatory characters in shabby bowlers hunting for prey, turned into a hothouse where plants of unimaginable beauty thrived in the steamy air. There are no bars on the windows; there are no documents waiting to be numbered with a red pencil. What addenda? What codicils? This is a green lawn. And yellowed, musty ornaments on the wall sprout new, tender leaves, spiral runners cling to the trellis and form an attractive bower. Mr. Syrovy officiates in a greenhouse, and flowers scatter pink leaves upon his head.

4   "So why don't they move?" Mother grumbled. "All you hear is moving, moving, but in the meantime they're still squatting in my house. Who needs them? Let 'em go to their flatfoot if they're so wild about him."

"They won't move," Father said; "who'd move nowadays. They know perfectly well that they'd never have it so good as they do here."

He got up and emptied his pipe into the coal bin.

"I don't want them here," his wife continued, "I could get good money for these rooms. Only today some gentlemen came looking for a place. . ."

"It's better if they stay. I don't want strangers in the house. It would bring disorder. Like downstairs, the Bednar place. Their tenant hung himself, and on Christmas Eve, too. He bought himself a quarter kilo of salami, ate it, and then hung himself . . . That's how it goes. Now the Bednars have problems. They've got to keep trudging to the police, report to all sorts of offices. It's unfair. That's the trouble with strangers. A stranger has no consideration."

"Everybody doesn't hang himself," countered Mother; "there are decent gentlemen, too. The teacher that used to live at the Bednars still remembers them; the other day they got a beautiful letter from him. Some tenants work out well and some don't."

"You keep on babbling and there's no end to it. Silly woman! Once they leave, who's going to read the paper to me? You know that I'm practically blind. I keep seeing red and green spots before my eyes. But of course, who cares about me!"

"There's no need to read the papers. You won't learn anything useful from them, anyway. Better mind your own business. . ."

"You starting up again? You silly old biddy! A hell of a lot you know about newspapers! Are you chasing me out of the house again? I see . . . You sure set a good example for the young folks. I'm not surprised they want to run away. This is one hell of a home."

That day Father didn't come home for lunch.

Chapter Eight

1   Winter came and went, and the hill in the suburb once more woke to life. Workers arrived and filled the house with bustle. Youths with paint-flecked faces brought in buckets of paint. The stove-maker kept sticking his crew-cut head into the stove. The plane kept whistling and sending out spirals of shavings. Then came a painter with a frost-bitten nose and his gray, limping helper. They set up their stepladder, placed stencils on the walls, and sang in harmony:

> *We don't want anything*
> *That belongs to others.*
> *We wish to live in peace*
> *With our German brothers.*
>
> *May both our peoples*
> *Flourish proud and free,*
> *But German subjects*
> *We shall never be.*

The policeman scurried among the workers, yardstick in hand. The drill-sergeant voice of his resounded off the bare walls.

But after the sun had set, the policeman put on his jacket and cap and went out. He stopped in front of the house and looked at the inscription above the doorway. The lettering was the handiwork of the plasterer, who also added a few stylized flowers:

> OH, HEART OF MAN,
> BECOME NOT THE HEART OF A PREDATOR

The policeman declaimed the inscription syllable by syllable, his eyes growing moist with emotion.

"I am a property-owner, I am a landlord," he said to himself, "and I'd like to see anyone dare stand in my way!"

2   Even the old house came to life with unusual bustle. They were moving the clerk's household belongings. "Heave — ho!" Hefty movers, their hair full of bits of straw, and cigarette butts stowed behind their ears, carried pieces of furniture from the third floor and set them down in front of the house, where a pair of horses with broad behinds pawed the ground impatiently.

The driver of the van, perched high up in the coachman's seat like an acrobat on an aerial bar, shouted: "Ho, Charlie! Hold it, or I'll belt you in the snout, you'll see!" The horse named Charles wiggled his ears, and leaning his head close to his neighbor whispered something to him.

Mother stood by the stove, stirring the soup and wiping her eyes.

Moved, she said to her daughter, who was packing her cooking utensils in crates, "Marie, don't forget us, and come and see us sometimes. You know that Dad is sick. It would mean a lot to him. And I bought you a few chunks of coal, so you'll have some to start with."

With a worried face, the clerk's father-in-law kept scurrying up to the second floor and down again, and like a circus clown he clumsily helped the movers lift pieces of furniture by the straps slung around their massive necks. The clerk stood in front of the house alongside the moving van, like a military guard next to a general's catafalque; he watched anxiously lest anything get broken.

After the last piece had been loaded, all the tenants who had been waiting in the hallway like a reserve regiment ran out into the street, and a sobbing chorus of farewell ensued. The tailor Samec stepped forward, ran his hand through his hair, and mumbled: "Stay well." The wife of the knife-sharpener came, surrounded by a throng of finger-sucking children; she carried the youngest on her back. She shouted: "Good luck and may the Lord bless you!" The knife-sharpener raised his gray head, bent all day over a buzzing wheel, and said: "Keep in touch!" They even carried down Mrs. Redlich, who had suffered a stroke; she watched the commotion with bulging eyes and kept mumbling: "Yes, yes, yes." Even the super's wife, whose husband had gone off to Russia and remarried, and whom the whole house had been calling a slut, kept wiping her nose with the back of her hand and crying bitterly. The tavern owner, bare-necked but wearing a dark jacket, came out from behind the bar, accompanied by the sour smell of stale beer, and shook the clerk's hand: "So you're leaving us, Mr. Syrovy? Right. All right. Stay well." Then he shouted to let his servant know that the sodawater had arrived.

The clerk was touched, and he felt his heart swell in his throat. He suddenly felt sorry to be leaving this old house, its peeling halls, its dark stairways where in the night young men were wont to press squealing servant girls against the railing; and the fourth floor, where an oil lamp blinked red under a gloomy crucifix. And somehow he even felt sorry about leaving the damp star on the ceiling and the felt slippers with the checkerboard design. He felt that a person who had been living so many years in a house became a part of it, and it seemed to him that the old house, too, was moved, knitting its brows and shouting: "Farewell, Mr. Syrovy!"

3   In the new house, the clerk's wife lit a fire in the stove. For the first time, smoke rose from the chimney like the smoke from Abraham's pyre, signaling that the new house had ceased to be a new house and had become a human dwelling. As soon as the rooms absorb their first odor of humanness, household spirits settle in the still-damp walls. But first, the construction spirits must depart; these are the beings that crackle menacingly in the floors, rustle in the bathroom, and relieve themselves with a crumbling sound inside the walls.

The fire crackled in the stove, the oven grew hot, and Mrs. Syrovy put on coffee for the painters. It is a sacrificial rite celebrating the agreement concluded between man and house. The painters sat down on the floor and dipped their mustaches into the cups. Then they wiped their mouths and said: "The Lord bless you."

Thereupon they climbed back on their stepladders and burst out in unison:

> He scorned the faithful love I bore him
> Betrayed his pledges with a smile
> I watched him get ma-air-air-ied
> And lead her past me down the aisle.
> Farewell, farewell, farewell. . .

4   Word got around that people were moving into the new house, and this excited the whole neighborhood. The news flew from one dwelling to another; alarum roused alarum, the way rebels in the mountains light a chain of fires to let the population know that the awaited hour has struck.

Old women ran out of gray houses, dragging aprons on the ground in their hurry; and beneath their blouses, their hanging bosoms bob back and forth like a bubble in a carpenter's level. Men lean out of windows, their pipes pointing at the ground like plumb bobs. Old men seat themselves in doorways and with toothless gums chew their cud.

The neighborhood stuck out its antennae and with huge interest fumbled through the kitchen cabinet, which was so heavy that four men cursing for all they're worth could barely drag it into the room. The onlookers leaning out of windows participated in the process of putting the cabinet down, though only by means of advice. Seeing the enormous piece of furniture, they gesticulated with their pipes and shouted: "Sideways! Boys, take it sideways!"

When the movers were finally done and had received their tips, they shifted their caps to the back of their heads and went across the street to the tavern, where they blew the foam off their beer mugs and declared: "Was that a bitch! Christalmighty! What a job!"

5   At last they released the rust-colored cat out of her basket. The cat had already prepared herself for the worst, never having experienced such a commotion before; she jumped out and landed in the middle of the kitchen, completely confused. Her eyes, stabbed through by the lines of her pupils, were as big and round as silver dollars. She sniffed the furniture with its shining white enamel, and having observed that the stove was lit, she calmed down and began the careful preening of her fur. She felt like resting after all her travails, but the multitude of strangers walking back and forth made her nervous. "What disorder," she thought to herself plaintively, "and what huge shoes they have! What if they step on my tail?"

And crouching low she slipped out and sprang to the top of the garden wall. There she curled up in a corner and sorrowfully recalled her warm old recess under the oven, which was a perfect spot for sweet musings about the vanity of everything but warmth.

6   They started to put the furniture in place. The policeman came and offered his help. He leaned his mighty shoulders against the cupboards and shifted the cabinet one way and the other. He, too, got a cup of coffee, which he drank standing up. He left with a doubt in his heart: whether it was proper for a landlord to do menial work for his tenants.

"They seem to think," he pondered angrily, "that I am some kind of a slave. But you're badly mistaken, my friends. Today I am the landlord, not anybody's servant. I don't begrudge you your government status. But don't push me too far, my dear boys, or I'll fix you. I am no pushover, make no mistake about it. And I don't need your coffee. Thank God I have enough to eat."

On the way he cast a sullen glance at his neighbor's house, which differed from his only by having a balcony. And he thought obstinately: "What do you need balconies for, you fool of a tailor!" He picked up a clod and tossed it at a group of sparrows gathered around a pile of horse droppings.

In the house, meantime, the brush was busily scrubbing and the broom was working furiously. The clerk took advantage of the confusion and disappeared. He told himself that he would look around his new surroundings. He set out at an easy pace along a factory wall which cut across a row of workers' tenements. The factory windows were broken, and through them resounded the dull hum of machines and the whine of transmission belts. Through an iron gate he saw the vast yard, where pieces of metal lay scattered about. Women, doubled over like the trunks of old willows, were collecting something or other and

54

putting it into burlap bags. A yellow structure, built in the kind of Moorish style often used for staff housing, was attached to the factory.

The wall was full of colorful posters. The clerk stopped in front of a green announcement, which stated:

> R. CASTONY
> Professor of Occult Sciences
> shall demonstrate the greatest wonders of ancient and modern ages.
> This event is sure to arouse the interest and amazement of the public
> as well as of international authorities.

Next to the Professor of Occult Science, the Vitezslav Halek Adult Education Society announced that on such and such a day there would be a performance of *Songs of an Old House*, a play in four acts. If you looked a bit lower, you'd see a mimeographed invitation for all and sundry to come to a public meeting to be held at the Old Gate Tavern . . . unbearable economic mis. . . strongly reject. . . expecting enthusiastic resp. . . The rest had been washed away by rain. From the Ringhofer factory a throng of workers came pouring out, wearing dented bowlers or flat caps pulled over their ears. They carried blue lunchboxes and oil-cloth shoulder bags.

When the clerk returned home, the cat was already at peace with the new circumstances; she sat under the well-scrubbed bench and purred. His wife, too, was seated, tired from the excitement and housework, and with dreamy eyes contemplated her new, shiny kitchen; her heart rejoiced that everything was back in order.

7   That night, their first night in the new house, the clerk gazed into the dark and listened to the vague rattle that seemed to come now from the attic, now from the direction of the bathroom. The spirit of the new house was moving into the walls. And that night the clerk had a dream that was so beautiful, words could never express it. He only remembered that the flowers in his garden bloomed with tiny glass bells, and when the breeze moved them they softly played the song "A Youth Came Riding." All his fellow employees gathered to hear the tune.

Then the web of the dream became tangled, and the clerk dreamt that he was walking down the street of some sort of town, watching his reflection in the windows. Then he noticed that his right earlobe was tiny, soft, and curled like a spring bud. He felt a peculiar pleasure in having such a delightful ear. When he woke up, he felt his ears and was ashamed to have been visited by such foolish fancies.

It was springtime, and the golden sun danced across the comforters. His wife sat in bed and said: "I seem to have dreamt of plums. That's a bad omen. To dream of plums means trouble."

"Oh no," answered the clerk, "plums mean sickness."

"At home they used to say plums bring trouble. I hope it doesn't come to pass."

"Anyway, that's just superstition," said the clerk. "Please fix my breakfast, sweets, or I'll be late."

Chapter Nine

1   And so began the history of the new house.

The black dog that had hoped to find a job as house watchman experienced disappointment: the policeman gave him to a young woman from Strasnice who ran a milk route. Hitched to a cart, the dog earned a hard living delivering milk to customers. His place was taken by a young bitch of a vague gray color. She would have liked to continue leading a life of playful puppyhood, but that is vouchsafed only to dogs of the wealthier classes. A poor dog has to begin worrying about making a living from earliest youth onward.

The bitch lay down in front of her little doghouse, determined to be obliging to the tenants and to try staying on good terms with everyone. Her name was Amina.

Early in the morning Amina let go with furious barking; her snout, raised high in the air, detected the sour smell of a beggar. A bleary-eyed old man, his face covered by moldy bristles, appeared in the door. He was drawn to the new whitewashed house like a wasp attracted by a rotting pear.

"Our Father, who art in heaven," he droned in a voice like an accordion. He hiccuped, wiped his nose with the back of his hand, and continued: "Hallowedbethyname, the best of luck to you, madam, I'm a cripple."

He was greeted with a certain amount of respect, for beggars were a rarity in this part of town. The first beggar in the house — that's a special occasion, like the first visit of a housing inspector. And then the flies arrived, determined that from this day on they would serve as members of the household. Their interest was especially aroused by the glass pendants of the chandelier. They gathered on the ceiling and helped to pass the time by rubbing one leg against the other.

2　　On the following day, a worldly type in an elegant, sporty suit approached the house, jumping over the leftover piles of building materials. Trying to keep a precarious balance, he slowly crossed over a puddle of oozing clay by means of a wobbly plank. The fellow had an English-style mustache and a briefcase under his arm. His melancholy eyes were full of a determination to persist and not to be deterred by any insult or injury.

The clerk had hoped at first that he might escape him; he kept hiding like a heretic at the time of the Counter Reformation. But the worldly type finally cornered him. He sat down in the kitchen, facing the clerk, and spread a sheaf of papers before him. In a monotonic, mechanical voice he pointed the way to the maxim that no matter how careful we might be, the danger of fire was ever present. And as Mr. Syrovy no doubt knew from the press and from personal experience, criminality was rising to a frightening extent, and anyone mindful of his interests should make certain to have his property insured against theft. The man was hard to resist; the clerk signed a contract.

After the agent had left, the clerk berated his wife: "Once again we're throwing good money out the window. Do you have to let in everybody who rings the doorbell? We don't have money to burn!"

"Who asked you to buy insurance? *You* signed the paper, not *me*. I didn't say a word! Why do you always blame me?"

The couple kept arguing and reproaching each other. But then they made peace, and agreed that even insurance may turn out to do some good.

3   That same day a short fellow, dressed in a rust-colored overcoat and wearing a brass tack in his ear, called out from the hallway: "Hey! Do you need a sewing machine?"

"We already have a sewing machine," answered Mrs. Syrovy.

"But I have extremely reasonable sewing machines," answered the man with the brass tack.

"Don't need any."

"But I have really fine sewing machines."

"We have one, why buy more?"

"I carry all the top brands of sewing machines. Quality guaranteed. Just take a look at this brochure."

"I'm satisfied with my machine."

"You can pay in monthly installments, you won't even feel them."

"Another time, mister."

"My goodness, madam, I almost forgot! How about coal? I sell it in bags and in bulk."

"We have plenty."

"Confound it! This isn't my morning! But lady, let me tell you — our coal is outstanding, it burns all by itself, really economical coal, a real miracle, madam! Every kind of coal — Ostrava coal, brown coal, black coal — you'll thank me, lady! And what about coke, briquettes, anthracite?"

"We've got plenty of everything."

"But how about cleaning powder — I bet I guessed right this time! No? Really? Come on! But wait a minute! I'll bet you can use some laundry powder, especially if it's our

Housewife's Delight brand — works fast, gentle on delicate clothing."

"For the time being I'm well supplied," Mrs. Syrovy said quietly.

"I don't seem to be having much luck today. Oh well, what can you do. Well then, goodbye, good luck to you, and when you need anything just call on me; you know that I'll give you good service." The rust-colored overcoat flitted off and disappeared like a fish in a pond.

4   The clerk came home for lunch, took off his coat, and sat down at the table. His wife, bathed in the red glow of the oven, ministered to various pots and pans and recounted the day's events.

Her adventures were simple. Circumstances related to shopping were sufficient to ignite her fantasy; she grew lively, describing the prices of necessities.

"There are several merchants on the street. The widow Malecek has the biggest shop. But I was told that she's expensive and not too good. I shopped at Mr. Stein's. He is pleasant and polite. You can't tell from the outside the kind of business he has. His shop is small, but he's got everything. That's the place that has a pair of bedroom slippers hanging by a string over the entrance. He asked me if we have any children. 'That's too bad,' he said, 'because children make for family happiness.' "

"Children. . ." grumbled the clerk. "I'd love to have children. But the circumstances aren't right for that now. When I get a promotion at the office, then maybe. . . A merchant like that has no idea what real life is all about. He'd love his customers to have children; it's good for business."

"He told me: 'I hand out free fairy-tale books for

children. But as it is, there is nothing I can do for you.' And he kept on making jokes. Such a merry fellow. . ."

"What fairy tales?" said the clerk, stirring his soup. "Who needs fairy tales? The soup needs salt."

"Here, help yourself. I'm glad the oven is working. Do you hear it humming? Like a steam engine. At ten o'clock I lit the fire and dinner is already done. And by the way, I ran into the landlady," the wife continued, secretively lowering her voice.

"Well?"

"She no longer calls me 'Madam.' She simply said: Good morning. They have our money, so they don't need to Madam me any more."

"That's enough!" the clerk said brusquely. "I told you before, I won't stand for any kowtowing. Hold yourself back. Don't lord it over them. I can't stand that."

"I have no interest in lording it over anybody. I just mentioned it. She simply nodded her head when she passed me. I didn't even stop to talk to her."

The clerk finished his dinner, picked up an almanac, and stretched out on the couch.

"Now for a bit of rest," he said with satisfaction.

Chapter Ten

1   Toward the end of the week the house got some new tenants. A one-legged veteran, who ran a newsstand under the arch of the viaduct, moved into the tiny upstairs garret. A peasant cart pulled up and, in addition to his furniture, unloaded a pale wife, a cage with a canary, and an accordion.

The policeman came, glanced at the furniture, with an expert eye examined the veteran's belongings, and said to Mrs. Syrovy: "Well, here they are, we're stuck with them. I took them in, so to say, out of pity. They kept begging and pleading with me that they had no place to live. So I thought to myself: what the devil! I am softhearted. The minute I saw their stuff I knew they were riffraff. Well, so be it . . . If they don't behave, out they go."

"Their furniture is made of soft wood," Mrs. Syrovy remarked.

"You don't have to pay any attention to them," the policeman concluded. "You're a better class of people; this is no proper company for you. And besides, if he ever decides to play that accordion at night, let me know; I don't tolerate any racket in the house. When it comes to disorderly tenants, I can be a real louse."

The policeman spat and left.

"Listen," said the clerk, when he learned of this conversation, "I won't stand for any gossip. The one-legged fellow hasn't done me any harm. I want to be on good terms with everybody. They may be perfectly decent people."

"But I didn't say anything different," his wife protested.

"You just said their furniture was made of soft wood. You can't deny that."

"And what's so bad about that?"

"I forbid you to pay any attention to other people's furniture. It starts with the furniture and ends with God knows what . . . I know that from experience. There is a lawsuit before our court, involving a landlord and a tenant, which has been dragging on for thirty years. And you know how the whole case started? The two parties quarreled because their maids didn't keep the doors shut . . . And that's how it goes."

"Don't talk so much," the wife brushed him aside, "and help me move this wardrobe. It's a wonder where all this dust comes from."

"Oh Lord," moaned the clerk, throwing up his hands, "another chore. Do you have to keep on cleaning and cleaning? Lord, will there never ever be any peace. . ."

2   The apartment on the ground floor was finally occupied, by a blond-haired fellow. He didn't wear a necktie but an open shirt with Slavic embroidery; and a pince-nez sat on his nose. He brought his wife, a lady with brown, kindly eyes.

He bowed and said: "I am technical teacher Soltys, and this is my wife."

The woman smiled, revealing her bright pink gums.

"This year we're having a fine spring," said Mr. Soltys; "of course we did have a few snow showers, but you have to expect that in April. . ."

"Yes, of course," the clerk nodded.

"The main thing is that we finally have a roof over our heads. We had a lot of trouble finding a place to live. We had to keep postponing our marriage. Now we have a place of our own, but of course this required great financial sacrifice. We thought about it for a long time, but then Grandpa Hynek appeared to us and advised us not to hesitate and to rent the apartment. Grandpa Hynek was a very sensible man. . ."

Then he fell silent, uneasily trying to come up with something else to say. Nothing occurred to him, so he bowed and left, followed by his wife.

"Their bedroom is all in white," the clerk's wife said after they had departed, "but I must admit I don't like it very much. The beds have carved headboards, and that's not practical, because dust settles in the grooves."

"That again? I asked you the other day to ignore other people's furniture," the clerk responded, frowning, "but you don't listen to me. Woe is me! I'm afraid evil things are in the offing."

"But what in the world did he mean when he talked about Grandpa Hynek?" he mused after a while. "He said that Grandpa Hynek appeared to them . . . I don't understand what he meant by that. . ."

"Oh, I suppose they asked his advice," the wife answered; "it's always good to get advice before spending such enormous sums of money . . . I wish I knew how much they paid the policeman. If they paid less than us, it was very clever of them."

3   The clerk stood on the terrace in his shirt-sleeves, enjoying the spring sunshine. The policeman was working in the garden; he was turning the soil over and carrying compost back and forth in a basket strapped to his back.

On seeing the clerk he stopped, wiped sweat off his forehead, and smiled.

"Well," he said with satisfaction, "my house is now full. One thing less to worry about."

"But I was under the impression," the clerk said, surprised, "that you would live here yourself . . . You built yourself a house, but you didn't move in."

"What an idea!" the policeman answered. "Is this my kind of place to live? No siree, I couldn't possibly afford to pay such high rents. Where would I end up? Oh no, not on your life!"

He bent down to pull up a root sticking out of the ground. Some loose soil trickled to the ground with a rustling sound.

"My landlady, too, thought that I'd move out once I had my own house. But I never dreamed of doing that. So she went ahead and sued me. That's what people are like nowadays. When you get to know me better, you'll put my picture in a gold frame. She slapped a suit on me, but it didn't do her any good. I won't budge from there, so help me God. Her: 'You'd love to pay a small rent and take in a big one.' Me: 'That's right, my good woman, that's how the world operates these days.' Poisonous old hag! But she won't outsmart me. I've been around."

"Some people have no consideration," said the clerk.

"Do it to me and I'll do it to you," the policeman continued. "If you treat me right, I'm your man. . ."

He picked up the basket and said: "If anyone thinks they can get the better of me, they'd better think again . . . I know what the world's about. You've got to get up early in the morning to get the better of me. . ."

And he went off to get more compost, fully pleased with himself.

4   The clerk remained standing a while longer and then walked to the back of the house to have a look at the yard. On seeing him, Amina let out a peculiar moan, jumped up, and struggled against the chain.

"Good dog, gooooood, yes, very good," the clerk cooed, rubbing the dog's neck.

This show of esteem made Amina lose every bit of her mental balance; she rolled over on her back and comically raised all fours in the air.

"A smart dog," said the policeman, who had just entered the yard in order to split some wood. "I got her from the gardener. She'll be a good watchdog. Amina," he commanded, "show the gentleman your tricks. Shake hands! . . . Well, how about it? I said shake hands!"

Amina sat down on her haunches, raised herself, and screwing up her face she waved her front legs.

"That's remarkable!" said the clerk. "And who taught her that?"

"Nobody," the policeman declared proudly; "she learned it all by herself. A smart dog; does anything but talk . . . . I have to put her somewhere else, however. I'll fix her up a doghouse on the terrace, because right here there'll be rabbit cages."

"And where will the poultry be?"

"Here, too, in the yard."

"But will there be room for the poultry of all the tenants?"

"What do you mean?" asked the surprised policeman. "You want to raise poultry? That won't be possible."

"But surely. . . " the clerk objected shyly, "it's in our contract. . ."

"In the contract. All sorts of things are in the contract."

The policeman smiled and pulled his tenant confidentially closer, by his lapel. "You mustn't take it too literally.

66

I thought the matter over and decided that it's impossible. Poultry is the cause of all sorts of misunderstanding and squabbles in a house. Believe me, I've had lots of experience. The birds get out into the garden, cause all sorts of damage, and then there's shouting and unpleasantness. And I don't hate anything more than dissension in the house. I always say: harmony in the house, reaching out a helping hand, that's what I like to see . . . All the other tenants are in accord. I explained everything to them and they don't want any poultry or rabbits."

The clerk listened with his head bowed and kept saying: "Yes, yes, of course, except. . ."

"There! You see!" the policeman exclaimed jovially. "I knew that we two would always be in agreement!"

He lit a cigarette and went to the cellar for a hatchet. On the way, he said to himself: "Poultry? Ha! They'd like to take advantage of my better nature. But I said: No. Shut up and off you go! I am the landlord!"

Chapter Eleven

1 Spring invaded the suburb. Rich green covered the hillsides. The turf was bright with the women's colorful skirts; mothers brought out their children to soak up the sun. Adolescents spread out blankets and enthusiastically played one game of cards after another. Old people stretched their limbs and, puffing on their pipes, engaged in long-winded conversations about the past and found fault with contemporary conditions. In the gardens, shiny blackbirds courted females, emitting deep, oboe-like tones. Everywhere there was commotion and excitement. Barefooted children held hands, danced in a circle, and intoned in off-key voices: "I have a spotted doggie, he's guarding my jet-black horse. . ." Park watchmen, their chests swelled by official responsibilities, patrolled the greenery and kept a sharp eye out for malefactors.

People scurried up and down the street carrying buckets of water from the public pump. They watered their plants and dug their soil with expressions of deep concern. They fussed about their little gardens, which they had artfully established on the stony slopes.

The policeman worked in his own garden and chatted with the clerk. "This," he said, "is where your beds will be. I picked out the best spot for you, to show you how much I respect you; it will have sun the whole day long. The teacher will have the plot next to yours. As for those people," and he pointed disparagingly toward the garret, "they'll have a piece of ground in front of the house. Any bit of soil is wasted on them. They pay the lowest rent and yet they put on airs like they're doing us a favor. She, especially, has a sour face. My wife thinks this woman may be waiting for us to greet her first, but in that case she'll have a long wait . . . If you'd like, I'll lend you some tools so you can get started."

2   The clerk took the hoe and started digging so energetically that he was soon out of breath. The policeman went back to his own work. Bending close to the ground, he crumbled clods of soil in his hand, picked up bits of glass and metal, and threw them over the fence. He felt all his sinews swell with the sense of ownership; his chest filled with pride and he talked to himself:

"This is my garden. Here, in this bed, I'll cultivate radishes. They aren't filling, but they're good to munch on after supper, for they purify the blood. Over there I'll grow my celery, the leaves of which give such a nice flavor to potato soup. This entire bed is reserved for cabbage; when cabbage is properly prepared, it's almost as filling as meat. Here and there I'll put in some flowers, to satisfy my need for beauty. The middle of the beds will be decorated with carnations and pansies. Such flowers can be obtained very cheaply from the gardener. I'll put in a few rose bushes, too, to enhance the beauty of the garden. I must see to it that the tenants plant fruit trees and gooseberry bushes around their plots. They'll become mine once the tenants move out. I've got too much on the ball to buy seedlings with my own money. This way I'll save a few pennies. It's a small profit, but a profit. And there's no need for us to use up all the vegetables ourselves. We'll sell whatever's left. Profit once again.

"I'll put up cages and huts, where I'll raise chickens and rabbits. There'll be no need to buy meat. I can't afford to buy any meat now, because the bank is pressing me hard for interest payments. We won't eat chicken ourselves; that's too expensive a dish for us. But we'll eat up all the eggs at home; that's profit, too. And I'll sell rabbit skins; a penny here, a penny there. It all adds up.

"I have a family. My wife sews diligently and my possessions expand. I have children, but they don't earn anything as yet. The boy should get a job where he's paid right from the start so that he can bring home some money. I have a father who helped me to build the house. Now I have to treat him carefully, otherwise he might want something from us. Mother is eternally hungry. It's amazing how ravenous she's getting with the passing years. She'll do the laundry for us; but we'll have to lock up the food. Anyway, I'll ask my brother-in-law to contribute to the upkeep of his mother-in-law. It's his duty to honor his wife's mother.

"I have tenants who are subject to my wishes. They are under my rule, for it is the duty of tenants to be quiet, follow my directions and regulations, and show me respect. I am no longer just a policeman, but a landlord; and it is only proper that the tenants be the first to salute me when we meet, rather than wait for my greeting. The tenants will keep bringing me their rent, which will lower the debt I owe the bank, so that in a few years the house will be mine, free and clear. People will say: 'Just think, an ordinary policeman and yet how far he has risen. . .' "

He circled the house, read the inscription: 'Oh, heart of man, become not the heart of a predator!' and said to himself: "A beautiful motto and a fine house. This house belongs to Jan Faktor, Police Sergeant."

3   The clerk came in from the garden and sat down on the bench by the stove. His arms hung limp by his side; his back hurt from the unaccustomed exertion; his palms had turned rough from the limey soil, and they burned. He was gloomy and his throat was dry.

"How is the gardening coming along?" his wife asked.

"So-so," the clerk said wearily. "It's hard labor, I'm surprised how tough it is . . . I can't make any headway. I kept digging in one spot. The ground is dry and hard as a rock."

"The policeman tricked us," said his wife: "he promised us half the garden, but gave us only an insignificant little bed. That's not fair and square."

"He's right," said the clerk, sighing heavily: "he knows perfectly well that I could never manage cultivating half the garden. It's unbelievable . . . I dug into that damned ground as hard as I could, and nothing came out except a few little clods. I'm not a laborer, after all . . . office work is all I'm good for. Oh Lord, my body aches, my head burns . . . I hope I don't get sick. I don't take proper care of myself. . ."

"Hmm," the wife responded, "and where will you plant the saffron? Where will our monks-hood be? You said the first row will be taken up by miniature hyacinths . . . And what about the perennials?"

"Perennials, perennials!" the clerk exploded. "Your eternal perennials! Noble plants require rich soil. But this isn't soil . . . it's a kind of dead dirt. A desert, where even henbane would call it quits . . . It's easy for you to talk, but my arms are ready to fall off. What misery!"

"You kept on babbling," countered the wife, "about how you'd start a new life . . . 'In my free moments I'll devote myself to gardening. I'll obtain technical information, and study it diligently. . .' "

"Leave me alone, will you!" the clerk exclaimed angrily.

" 'Oh, how I look forward to it,' you said. 'I'll dig and hoe,' " the wife continued mercilessly; " 'my muscles will round out, my face will take on a bronze sheen. . .' That's what you said. Next time you'd better keep your mouth shut."

"Woe is me!" moaned the clerk. "I don't have a moment's peace . . . Garden! I don't want to hear that word, you understand! To the devil with it. I wasn't born to struggle against harsh nature. . ."

"We'll have to hire somebody," the wife pondered gloomily. "Again, more expenses. But the landlord won't get our garden as a gift. To pay such a high rent and not even enjoy the garden? Not on your life."

But then an idea occurred to her. She picked up the hoe and spade and proceeded to work on the flower-beds till sundown.

"There," she said with satisfaction, examining the finished job. "There won't be any need for hired help. The first year we'll plant peas. Peas break up soil like dynamite. And the following year we can grow something else."

4   The evening air was full of spring. The hillsides smelled of fresh grass and dew. The street resounded with loud conversation; everyone wanted to enjoy the beautiful evening. The sounds of an accordion wafted from the field. A man's voice sang longingly: "Don't mind the shower, give me a flower, give me a pink flower, girl. . ." The song was interrupted in the middle by loud female screeching.

Mrs. Syrovy said: "We could go out for a walk."

"Not today," moaned the clerk; "I ache all over."

"Nonsense. You're just not used to this life. It will pass."

They stepped out of the house and headed toward the fields.

On seeing the couple, the grocer took off his cap and exclaimed: "How do you do, and there you go. Good evening, good evening! Out for a stroll?"

"Yes, a stroll," answered Mrs. Syrovy.

"Yes, well, I believe it is a good evening for a stroll."

"Are those the policeman's tenants?" the grocer's neighbor inquired.

"Yes," the grocer answered, cleaning his pipe. "His name is Syrovy."

"And what does he do?" the neighbor asked.

"You got me there. Works at the courthouse or something."

"Real high-class people," the neighbor remarked. "The way they strut along. Did you see her patent-leather shoes?"

"It's not quite like it seems," the neighbor's wife joined the conversation. "I was told by Mrs. Faktor that they don't even have a housekeeper. So what sort of upper crust can they be, if they don't even have a housekeeper. It's obvious they're not swimming in money."

"I don't know anything, I don't listen to anything, I don't tell any tales," said the grocer, maintaining a tradesman's caution. "They shop in my place, pay cash, and don't run up a tab like so many others. So why should I snoop around? I mind my own business. It wouldn't do me any good to stick my nose where it doesn't belong."

"But I was just talking to make conversation," said the neighbor's wife.

"Sure, sure," the grocer mumbled, and he trudged on home.

Chapter Twelve

1   Mrs. Syrovy was sweeping the floor, and this bothered the cat; the cat was especially upset that her mistress had pulled the bench away from the stove.

All in all, it was a beautiful morning, and the cat was lured outdoors by the white sun. She stretched out on the porch and began to preen her fur, which was matted with soot. She had already found the new neighborhood to her taste and wandered many a night over the roofs, searching for adventure. She managed to smooth an unruly tuft that had been sticking out from her head. And then her attention was caught by some sparrows hopping on the lawn and looking for food. She half closed her eyes in an innocent way, as if she meant to indicate: "Please don't think, you avian riff-raff, that I take any interest in you," and looking sideways she dragged her belly on the ground and crept with an indifferent mien toward the group of birds.

The dog in the yard got wind of her and pricked up her ears with a quiet whine. All of a sudden she let out a terrific roar and threw herself upon the cat, black gums bared. The cat nimbly spun around and sank her claws right in the dog's nose. Amina moaned and resumed her attack with redoubled fury. The cat leaped onto a wall and arched her back; her fur stood on end and her green eyes looked angry and threatening.

"I'll tear you apart," Amina bellowed, beside herself with fury. "I'll tear you to pieces, you stinking cat . . . How dare you enter the yard! This is no place for you. The yard is my property and not yours. My master doesn't allow cats to tramp across our yard. I won't permit it! Scram!"

"I'm not scared of you," hissed the cat. "You leave me alone or I'll let you have it . . . I forbid you to insult me! We are tenants and we have a right to use the yard. . ."

"The yard is ours, you understand?" the dog wheezed furiously. "We insist on discipline. We can be real bastards when it comes to rebellious tenants. I'll grab you by the neck . . . miserable scum . . . I won't put up with you! I won't permit it!"

"Why is the dog carrying on like that?" Mrs. Syrovy wondered, and she went out to the yard.

"Amina, how dare you!" she reproached the dog. "I'll whack you if you don't leave the pussycat alone. Sit!"

Frightened, Amina crawled into her doghouse with a whimper.

"I made a mistake," she admitted to herself, full of shame. "I'm guilty of misfeasance. How strange people are! Cats smell so awful, yet people love them. What strange goings-on . . . So the cat belongs to the lady and must be treated with respect. Oh well, never again . . . what do I care? Let her walk in the yard. She isn't in my way."

"Miss," the dog called out courteously, "I was only joking, please forgive me. If you wish to go for a walk, go ahead by all means . . . I won't bother you."

But the cat puffed herself up, gave the dog a contemptuous glance, and left with an insulted air. She searched out a spot in the sun, curled up, and fell asleep with memories of last night's adventures.

At noon, when Mrs. Syrovy brought the dog some leftovers from lunch, Amina said to herself: "They've already forgotten the episode. They're not angry, thank God. . ."

Hungrily crunching on the bones, she thought: "Tenants

come in handy, very handy . . . That's good . . . Profit once again!"

2   Mother asked her husband to go and see how the young couple was doing in their new house.

"I'm lonely without them," she sighed. "I can't tell you how much I miss them! It's true he never said much, but I miss him all the same. He would always sit over there on the couch, in the corner, never said anything, just stared at the ceiling . . . I wonder how they're doing. They're among strangers, the poor things; they have no one to take care of them."

Father threw up his hands: "Among strangers! What strangers? You can find good people everywhere, remember that! But we won't abandon them. I'll pay them a visit and take care of everything. . ."

 "You're different, you're a worldly person. You've traveled abroad. But Syrovy is something of a homebody. You'd better pay them a visit, dear . . . I baked them a cake and packed some goose giblets. The poor things need a bit of a treat in that out-of-the-way place."

Father set out with determination. He took a streetcar and got off in the suburb. He had to ask a lot of people for directions before he found the policeman's house, and this filled him with irritation.

"What an idea," he thought angrily: "to settle down on such a miserable hill. It makes a person's head swim. Like a fortress. They probably did it on purpose, to keep us from visiting them. Very well . . . Just as you wish. You don't care for us — we can live without you, too. . ."

On the stairs he brushed against the policeman and asked him whether Mr. Syrovy lived there.

The policeman answered: "He lives here, and what do you want with him?"

Father measured him with a proud glance and wondered: "Should I tell him off, or shouldn't I?"

He said at last: "Mr. Syrovy is my son-in-law."

"Ah, I see!" the policeman burst out heartily. "So you happen to be his father-in-law?" He looked him over and ascertained the presence of a gold pince-nez attached to a gold chain; he concluded that the in-law must belong to a better class of people. He felt the urge to show off.

At that moment a young fellow wandered in with a package under his arm, and shuffled toward the door.

"Hold it! Where to?" the policeman stopped him brusquely.

"Does a Mister Saleny live here?" the youth asked in a hoarse voice. "If he does, he's supposed to come see Mr. Lacina right away."

The policeman sensed that the in-law was watching him. He threw out his chest and bellowed: "Get the hell out of here! There is nobody named Saleny around here. This house belongs to Police Sergeant Faktor. I am Police Sergeant Faktor. This is my house and my garden. If I ever catch you here again, I'll grab you by the collar and throw you down the stairs. Away with you, you punk, before I thrash you!"

The frightened youth slinked away like a kicked dog.

"That's all we need," the policeman turned to the father-in-law: "to have a bunch of street urchins promenading through here. You know, sir, I am tough. I don't tolerate any hoodlums around here. The tenants are under my protection; they are as safe as in a prison. I drive everyone away. . .!"

The policeman bared his teeth and stamped his feet. He was satisfied with his performance.

3   "You seem to have an energetic landlord," Father said to his daughter; "he is very strict. He chases criminals from his doorstep, which I approve of. Mother will be glad to hear that you are in good hands. She is sending you a few goodies for the household."

"Thank goodness!" the clerk's wife exclaimed, examining the giblets with an expert eye. "I couldn't think of anything to cook for tomorrow!"

"We'll take care of you as best we can," Father said; "you can depend on us. But don't ever forget that you have duties toward us as well. Yesterday I had awful heartburn. I believe," he lowered his voice mysteriously, "I believe that my innards have dried out. My stomach needs a bit of greasing. I asked the doctor about it. I said to him: 'I have a stitch in my side, what could that mean?' 'That's nothing,' the doctor said, 'it will go away.' And he gave me some drops. I don't think he knows what he's doing. If I had the money, I'd visit a foreign specialist. But as it is, I'll perish on account of poverty . . . Ah, here's Jindrich! What's new at the office, Jindrich?"

The clerk took off his coat and replied that everything was the same as always.

"Yes," Father sighed, "and down there it's a mess again."

"Down where?" asked the clerk.

"In China. Squabbling all the time. First one side wins, the next day the other side. A person can't make any sense of it. Of course, when I was young I had a good head for politics. Nowadays my eyes are so weak I can't even read the paper. Samec the tailor reads me the paper. . ."

He grew pensive and reached for the doorknob: "And the French cabinet resigned . . . What's behind it, I wonder? There's all sorts of chicanery. Nowadays you can't trust anybody. They tell me: 'Come to the meeting. You haven't come to a meeting in ages.' What's the problem? Can't you start a meeting without me? Some way to run an organization . . . And they raised our water tax. If I had a pen I'd write a letter to the editor about it. And here, too: your stairs are in terrible shape. The housing authority should be told about it; it's a threat to life and limb. They should make your landlord do his duty. Take money, yes; fix the stairs, no. A good thrashing is needed. . ." the old man grumbled as he shuffled out the door.

Chapter Thirteen

1   "Are you watering the garden?"

"I'm watering, I'm watering."

"Good. There's need of moisture. It's been ages since the last rain."

"Exactly . . . The earth is thirsty."

The policeman dipped his watering-can in the barrel and sprinkled the soil. In the arc of the water droplets, the sun's rays broke into a rainbow fan.

"And how about you, what are you up to?" he asked his neighbor, Mecl.

Mecl the tailor was standing next to a pile of boards; with an expression of deep concentration, he was making measurements and drawing heavy lines with a blue pencil.

"I'm just constructing a little gazebo," he answered, "a little garden house for the children. Next month my daughter is getting hitched. She always wanted a gazebo, so here it is. You know what children are like, you've got to please them." "Is that so?" the policeman called out sweetly. "Your young lady is about to get married? You must be very happy!"

"I am glad, I am sad," said the tailor, making a fatherly face.

"Gazebo. . ." the policeman grumbled to himself. "I also wanted to build a gazebo, and now I can't. That fool of a tailor would think that I was trying to copy him . . . He says his daughter is getting married. But the way she slept around with officers in the old Austrian days, that he doesn't boast about . . . And the older one had a bastard child . . . We know all about you, mister tailor . . . You won't fool us with your gazebos. We'll have to tell his father-in-law about the way that needle-pusher brought up his daughters . . . You're not going to lord it over us, no sir!"

Then the policeman went to the cellar to fetch his masonry tools, for he intended to cement his yard.

On the way, he met the news dealer's wife carrying a pitcher of milk.

He gave her a sly wink and said: "Would you do me a favor?"

"What is it?"

"Nothing much . . . Just stand in the garden and shout: 'Captain of the sixth artillery regiment. . .' That's all."

"Why should I shout 'Captain of the sixth artillery regiment?' I don't understand."

"I'll explain it to you. It's just a kind of joke."

"Well, I don't know. . ." the woman said uneasily. "I'd be ashamed. I couldn't do that, Mister Landlord, I have a very shy nature."

"But there's nothing to it . . . All right, so just call out

'That Hungarian lieutenant!' You'll see Mecl get all excited."

"I mustn't shout at people, Mister Landlord; my husband would never allow it."

"But I allow it. And I am the landlord."

"Even though you're the landlord, you mustn't ask me to do something that isn't right."

"Very well, my little woman," the policeman grumbled sourly, "I won't say any more . . . Of course, I know perfectly well that you spilled paint all over the stairs. . ."

2   Mrs. Syrovy told her husband: "He said that it's all right for me to dump the garbage in the yard. He said that things haven't been quite organized as yet and that he would get rid of the garbage himself. I told him not to bother, I didn't mind taking the can to the garbage cart. But he answered: 'Oh no, you're frail, Mrs. Syrovy; you have to take care of yourself. Don't waste your strength on the garbage.' "

"It's obvious," the clerk retorted, "that our landlord is a considerate man. I give him credit for that."

"But he no longer calls me 'Madam,' only 'Mrs. Syrovy.' 'Mrs. Syrovy,' he said, 'you're so frail and have to take care of yourself.' "

"He doesn't call you 'Madam' any longer? That seems strange. Hmm. . . You haven't been gossiping about him, have you?"

"Me? God forbid! On the contrary . . . The news dealer's wife was telling me recently that the policeman's promotion is blocked because his wife is so jealous . . . But I said. . ."

"Just a minute," the clerk stopped her. "What was that you just said? That his promotion is blocked because his wife is jealous? What kind of nonsense is that? Promotions can be blocked only on the basis of a disciplinary hearing. And a disciplinary hearing is initiated as a result of various misdemeanors, such as carelessness in the performance of duty, gross subordination, and so on. Of course, the private lives of state employees are also subject to review. A government employee, such as for example myself, must behave decently and must be a model for his fellow citizens in all possible ways. But as far as jealousy is concerned. . . I never heard of anything like that . . . although of course a man's superiors would condemn any jealousy leading to public disturbance. But I see that you talk too much. What business is it of yours whether that landlord's wife is jealous or not?"

"But I didn't say anything," Mrs. Syrovy defended herself; "it was the news dealer's wife . . . I answered: 'Mrs. Krejz, I don't know anything and I don't pry into things that don't concern me. . .' She said that she didn't pry either, that she simply heard. . ."

The clerk stopped answering, having turned his attention to his stamp collection. His wife cleared away the dishes and put water on for coffee.

After a while, she said: "By the way, did you know that the landlord's wife had that boy while she was still single?"

"Who told you that?" the clerk asked nervously.

"She herself told me . . . The boy was already five years old when they got married."

"If she herself told you, then it's all right," the clerk calmed himself. "Now you keep quiet and make the coffee. All of us have our own troubles."

3   The policeman couldn't get his neighbor's gazebo out of his mind, and in the end he decided to build a table and bench and place them in the garden.

"It isn't much, a table and a bench," he mused, "and yet it's something. Let the tailor see my handiwork. After all, what's a gazebo? Just a bit of silly nonsense. But we can all sit on the bench, me, the wife, and all the tenants, and have a nice chat. Let people see the way I converse with my tenants. When good will rules a house, there is no need for gazebos. . ."

He carried out what he had planned. Out of some old crates he nailed together a table and bench, set them up in the garden and, in proud anticipation, peered over the fence to see what the neighbor would have to say to that. But he saw a sight that knocked the breath right out of him:

The tailor's daughter was sitting on a garden swing, ardently swinging to and fro, completely immersed in herself. It was evident that her family considered a swing a symbol of social superiority and bourgeois bliss; when the tailor started to build, it was decided in family discussions that a garden swing, above all else, would demonstrate that they were a better class of people.

The policeman was astounded, and his head filled with anger.

"A swing. . .!" he whispered in amazement. "What's this latest trick you're playing on me? Are you trying to ridicule me? What do you know about refinement, you miserable needlepusher! Do you think I can't afford a swing? A garden swing! . . . Imagine! But I know all about you. You won't get the best of me . . . I won't stand for such uppishness . . . and one day I'll make you pay for it."

But he forced his face into a good-tempered smile and called over the fence in a voice full of neighborly geniality:

"I see you're relaxing, Miss."

"Yes, relaxing," the young woman replied in a languid voice.

"Go ahead, swing away," the policeman continued in a fatherly tone. "It's pleasant to swing, to breathe fresh air . . . just keep on swinging . . . it's becoming to young ladies. . ."

The policeman's wife came with his afternoon snack.

"Look at this, Anastazie!" the policeman whispered furiously: "they bought a garden swing."

The policeman's wife glanced into the neighbor's garden, threw up her arms, and hissed: "A swing? You just wait. . ."

And she ran off to the grocer's.

4   Balmy dusk descended on the neighborhood. The sweet aroma of blooming trees and moist grass filled the air. The lamplighter walked from one streetlight to the next and lit the gaslamps with his long rod. In the windows curtains were drawn. Streets rang with the whooping of children and the laughter of women. The grunting sounds of gramophones resounded from cellar apartments.

A group of adolescents gathered around a youth with a guitar. An enormous moon, bloody and tragic-looking, floated up over the Jewish cemetery. Bluish smoke rose from chimneys up toward the starry sky. A man's voice sang out from the fields: 'They sit side by side in the green grove, they sit side by side and fight. . .' Grasshoppers chirped shrilly, and a nocturnal bird hooted like a factory whistle from the woods behind the brickyard.

The policeman went around to all his tenants with an invitation: "After supper, come and sit with us in the garden."

The news dealer finished supper, put on his wooden leg, and went outside with his wife.

Then came the clerk and Mrs. Syrovy.

At last they were joined by the teacher Soltys and his spouse.

"Now we're all gathered together," the policeman said with satisfaction. "We are seated together in harmony, like one big family . . . I feel like a father and you are the children entrusted to me. That's how I like it . . . In some places the tenants and the landlord fight like a bunch of gypsies. That's ugly. There's got to be give and take. And if any misunderstanding should arise among you, you can turn to me; I'll straighten it out. Come straight to me; and I'll be straight with you. I don't like talk behind people's backs. Loose talk leads to quarrels."

"It's a beautiful evening," the policeman's wife sighed dreamily.

"A beautiful evening," agreed the news dealer's wife.

"We've finally been rewarded with some lovely weather," the clerk said wistfully.

"And the heavenly vault arches over us," the teacher Soltys said in a mournful voice, "and God's eye looks down upon us . . . It almost makes a person faint to contemplate the dizzying depths of the heavens. . ."

This made them speechless.

The teacher continued: "If we consider that a ray of light takes hundreds of thousands of years before completing its journey from the constellation of Sirius all the way to us, our insignificance makes us tremble. . ."

The policeman mused: "I own a lot of six thousand one hundred and twenty square meters. I wonder if six thousand one hundred and twenty square meters of the sky which arches over my property belongs to me as well." But then he dismissed the idea, realizing that no profit was to be gained from the sky.

He said: "You told us, teacher, that a person trembles

over his insignificance. Yes . . . Some people are insignificant, others are not. I used to be insignificant.

"When I think of my younger days. . . Dad was a bricklayer, the house was full of children. They sent me out to learn the woodcarving trade; a stupid trade which doesn't pay anything. I couldn't get work and so I took any job I could. I ran a steam-shovel, I worked on construction gangs. And so I knocked about as best I could. Then came the time for military service. In the army I was quick to learn and I kept my nose clean, and so I kept advancing in rank. I was discharged without a single bad mark, and as a result of my good record I got a job with the police. . ."

Chapter Fourteen

1   "A star just fell," the policeman's wife whispered dreamily.

"The sky is cleaning itself," Mrs. Syrovy remarked.

"That's just a way of talking," the teacher explained; "actually it signals the destruction of some distant world."

"When I was a young flatfoot," the policeman resumed his tale, "I had the ambition to arrest a murderer . . . You know how eager young people are. And so one day I had an adventure . . . I'm standing at my post, keeping my eyes peeled. A man comes running up, terrified. 'Somebody's got killed at the Chimneysweep Tavern!"

"We run to the place. As you can imagine, this was just what I'd been hoping for. We arrive at the tavern and a group of fellows are seated at a table; as soon as they see me, they break into gales of laughter. 'Where's the body?' I ask. They laugh. 'One of our buddies got soused, that's all.' I saw that they'd pulled a joke on me. And I couldn't get angry, because they heaped more food and drink on me than I could handle. . ."

The policeman reached into his vest pocket, pulled out a cigar butt, and lit it.

He blew a smoke ring and immersed himself in recollections.

"All sorts of things have happened in the line of duty. One day I'm patrolling my beat in Mala Strana. Mr. Bem, who at that time ran the Golden Key winecellar, comes up to me. 'There's a man in my place, I'm pretty sure it's Sladecek. It's an extremely awkward situation for me. Please take him away, I don't want to have anything to do with him. I don't want any trouble, I just want him to leave the premises. . .'

Sladecek was a notorious thief of overcoats. I said to the tavern-keeper: 'I'll take care of it.' And he said: 'Please, I wouldn't want any unpleasantness. My place must be clean. My customers are for the most part respected people, government officials. They wouldn't like to find Sladecek among my guests.' And I say: 'Don't you worry.'

I go to the tavern and the barkeeper pours me a glass of wine. I look without looking. A man is sitting there. And would you believe it! It's really Sladecek. I wait until he steps out into the hall. Then I go up to him and say: 'You're Sladecek!'

'Who's Sladecek? I don't know any Sladecek.'

'Never mind. Come with me.'

I put handcuffs on him because I know what a crafty fellow he is.

Along the way he tells me: 'You're the first man who

ever managed to catch me. Until now no flatfoot ever got the better of Sladecek. . .'

The commissioner, who interrogated him, asked: 'Tell me, Sladecek, how many overcoats have passed through your hands?' 'I think it's been more than three thousand,' Sladecek said proudly. He later died of TB, in prison. . ."

2   "Yes. . ." the policeman sighed, "I've had some hard times . . . In the police department it was difficult at first. But then things improved when they noticed my adeptness at physical pursuits . . . At that time they were starting a police wrestling club. I joined and won many matches and prizes. But now I no longer do it. I realized I never got anything out of it. I'd sweat, while others got the praise and recognition. That's no good. Training and more training, the hell with that! But there was some profit in it, after all. They transferred me to the telegraph, and that's a lot easier and more comfortable assignment than chasing thieves and fighting with demonstrators. . .

"I was always very careful not to stay at one level but to keep advancing. People say: a flatfoot . . . Yes, a flatfoot . . . But just look at me now. I can speak with any gentleman as his equal. For I am a landlord. . ."

He got up, spread his legs wide, and swept his tenants with an imperious look. He tried to think of something else to say to reinforce his stature.

He said: "There was a time when I could down twenty-five beers at one sitting. . ."

"My oh my," the news dealer mumbled in amazement, "twenty-five beers, that's something!"

"Naturally, I couldn't do it now. I have to save money; I couldn't afford. . ."

"Aaaahhh," yawned the clerk. "I feel sleepy. It's about that time. . ."

"We've had a pleasant chat, but now we must go to bed," said Mrs. Syrovy.

The party broke up. Only the news dealer remained with the policeman.

"Mister landlord," he said cajolingly, "wouldn't you like to visit with us? A little game of cards. . .? My wife will make us some tea with rum. . ."

The policeman hesitated. Then he said: "I'd like to . . . But I haven't touched a card in ages. I don't know if I still know how to play. . ."

"Oh, go on," the news dealer wheedled, "an old soldier like you . . . Just for pennies. . ."

"All right," the policeman decided, "I'll get my brother-in-law and bring him along. We'll play . . . Why not. . ."

3   The policeman went to fetch his laconic brother-in-law, who was just getting ready for bed. The policeman asked him in a commanding tone to get dressed and ready for a game of cards.

The laconic man inwardly resisted: he didn't much care for cards and was afraid of losing. His eyes begged his wife for support.

But she said: "Go ahead, Alois . . . for the sake of good will. Perhaps he'll have a change of heart and pay the back wages he owes you. . ."

Muttering under his breath and crunching curses between his teeth, the in-law left his house. On the way they met the grocer, who was in the midst of locking up for the night.

"How lucky," said the policeman: "here's our fourth . . . Mr. Mejstrik, drop everything and come with us for a few hands of cards . . . No big deal, just for peanuts. Just for the fun of it."

The grocer thought: "What nerve! Just like that: go play

cards! As if I had nothing else to do. And I promised the wife that I'd fix the shelves for her. When will I get around to it? The devil take you, you tin-foil flatfoot. . .!"

But then he recalled that the policeman had once caught him doing business on Sunday, through the back door. And so he scratched the back of his head and said to himself: "It's no use. The bastard would give me a hard time. He'd remember and give me a fine. Nowadays policemen have all the rights. . ."

Aloud, he said: "Very well . . . I'll just fetch my pipe and be right back. . ."

4   The news dealer's wife stood by the stove and gloomily watched the guests, who were puffing on their pipes and fervently spitting on the floor.

"That'll be some mess to straighten up, God help us!" she grumbled silently. "I feel like sleeping, I can't keep my eyes open and I can hardly stand on my feet. What got into that man of mine? And they won't leave until I drag the chairs out from under them. . ."

The policeman was buoyant, for he was winning. He shuffled and dealt the cards in the practiced manner of an experienced player. The whole house shook as he pounded the table with his fist. Whenever he shouted: "My trick!" Amina answered with furious barking from the yard, for she thought that a brawl had broken out in the house.

When the gray morning finally dawned, he rose to his feet, sixty crowns to the good.

"How did you make out?" he asked his in-law.

The laconic man sniffed melancholically.

"I lost," he answered with a belch. "I lost over twenty crowns. Damn business. . ."

"That's because you're a fool," the policeman berated him, "you can't be trusted with money . . . That's why I held back your wages, because I know you can't handle money . . . And I am not about to hand you any business loans, either. My banknotes would curl up in fright."

He left his in-law and set out for home.

He saw the jack of spades dancing before his eyes, waving two swords. With his arrow, a cupid on a red ten was nailing a heart to a leaf-bedecked pole. A boy was holding a smoking pipe in his hand, while a seven of oaks grew out of his hat. A knave of clubs piped on a flute. The blue-eared ace of oaks held two escutcheons in its claws, its broad mouth open wide. The policeman ran his hand across his face to banish the image of the mustachioed king of diamonds, who had taken possession of his over-wrought nerves, for diamonds were his lucky suit.

His heart chimed merrily in his chest as he talked to himself:

"I really cleaned out that news dealer. I won sixty crowns. Sixty crowns is a respectable sum . . . For sixty crowns you can buy a shirt.

For sixty crowns you can get a kilo of sugar.

For sixty crowns you get almost two kilos of coffee.

For sixty crowns it's possible to have your shoes resoled.

If one currant bush costs six crowns, that means we could get ten currant bushes.

Sixty crowns covers household expenses for two days.

Sixty crowns equals six pairs of pigeons.

Sixty crowns buys me enough tobacco for two months.

People might think that sixty crowns doesn't mean anything, but look: for sixty crowns you can rent a plot of land and plant enough potatoes to last all winter.

I can spend the news dealer's sixty crowns and I don't have to spend my own sixty crowns. That means saving. That means profit. That's good! That's good!

The shiny crowns stick to me and call me 'sir'!

That's good!"

5   The news dealer's wife complained bitterly: "You men have no consideration. A gang of you get together and make dirt and disorder. Nobody cares about me. Next time I'll throw out the whole bunch of you. . ."

"Shush," hissed the news dealer, "that's foolish talk. I only did it for the sake of good will. After all, he's our landlord and a policeman. I myself don't care too much for cards. I too prefer to sleep. But you know as well as I do that he has a grudge against us because we only gave him a deposit of seven thousand crowns. I wanted to host him so that he'd stop calling us poor rabble. We need to humble ourselves, so he doesn't kick us out. . ."

"He'll kick us out anyway," his wife mumbled sleepily. "I know it perfectly well . . . he was overheard saying that we'll be the first to be heaved out as soon as the time comes . . . It was a waste for me to make tea with rum . . . We're only paying fifteen hundred a year, so he doesn't look on us with a kindly eye. And he won't let us keep rabbits, even though it's in the contract. . ."

"Be quiet, woman, and go to sleep. It's late. What do we care about rabbits . . . Good will is more important . . . We must be meeker than water . . . And not a word about rabbits, you understand. We are little people and have no way of defending ourselves. . ."

6   "Damn it. . ." grumbled the clerk, tossing from side to side. "It's after two and he still keeps yelling 'my trick, my trick' . . . what sort of business is that? I've taken a second dose of pills and I still can't sleep for all the racket . . . Isn't this supposed to be a policeman's house? The police are supposed to serve as a good example and to punish rowdy behavior . . . not to create a ruckus themselves. At night everyone's supposed to be asleep, except for people designated to stay awake . . . But that news dealer is egging the policeman on. I heard that news dealers are for the most part corrupt people . . . Wham! There he goes again, pounding the table and laughing till the windows rattle. This should be outlawed! My head is spinning from all this disturbance. . ."

The clerk got up and went to get a glass of water.

"He's playing cards with him," his wife said, "and yet he himself called the news dealer vermin that's got to go. He said it doesn't look good to have a news dealer in a building that houses a government employee and a teacher. And now he's keeping company with him. When he met me yesterday he said: 'I don't like tenants to visit one another . . . A tenant is supposed stay in his own place and mind his own business . . . If you happen to meet the news dealer's wife,' he said, 'just say hello and nothing else. Don't get into long conversations with her. That would detract from your dignity. And I don't tolerate a lot of fraternizing in my house. The tenants get into cahoots and start grumbling against their landlord. I see every-thing,' he said, 'and I pay careful attention. I've long had my eye on the news dealer's wife, because I know that she spreads gossip. . .' "

"Be quiet, woman, and go to sleep," her spouse remon-strated; "you know how we had to wrack our brains before we found a place to live. No more talk, it doesn't lead anywhere . . . Nowadays the landlord has all the rights. It behooves us to be patient . . . Don't talk to anybody and don't pay any attention to anybody . . . Oh, what a difficult position we're in. . ."

"We stuck twenty thousand into him, and now we can't budge . . . Twenty thousand, and it's still not enough for him. He has no right to forbid me to talk to anybody I choose . . . twenty thousand. . ."

"Twenty thousand," muttered the clerk, "exactly . . . Not another word . . . The policeman is right. There is no need to talk to others, no good will come of it . . . and now go to sleep. It's quiet upstairs, at last. . ."

Chapter Fifteen

1   Today the suburb gets up a bit later. If you look into the windows, you'll see men at their washstands, naked to the waist. Women in underwear run around the rooms. From the basement apartments comes the wheedling of children and irritable voices. A bald head leans out the window and calls out: "Manya! Manya! Get away from that puddle! Or I'll take off my belt. . ."

Two old women stand on the corner, chatting: "And so I dropped two eggs into the batter . . . two eggs . . . I gave her the whole plateful, and she says: Mom, I'd like another roll . . . oh sure, you're still starved . . . hahaha . . . she'd already gulped down five rolls and still it wasn't enough . . . I look at her and think: dear girl, God bless you . . . it's better when they stuff themselves than when they don't eat at all. . ."

"You said it," the other one agreed; "our little one is the same . . . and yet she's as thin as a rail."

The clerk stretched, yawned blissfully, jumped off the bed, and shuffled into the kitchen. It made him feel good to think that today was Sunday and that the weather looked so cheerful. He tried to sing some sort of operatic aria, but emitted a gargling sound as if his throat were blocked with grease.

"Get out of my way," said his wife. "I have loads of work to do. Get dressed and go out for a walk . . . Off with you."

"Marie," the clerk answered, "you're hard on me. But I'll do as you say. I'll go for a stroll and buy the paper. So be it . . . After lunch we'll read what's happened in the world. . ."

Humming and whistling to himself, he put on his Sunday suit and left the house.

2 Mrs. Syrovy was trying to solve the problem whether to make breaded cutlets or prepare cutlets *au nature,* when her father walked into the kitchen.

He remained standing by the door like a tramp, hat in hand.

"Good morning, Daddy," his daughter greeted him. "Why don't you come in."

The old man heaved a deep sigh.

"You won't chase me from your doorstep?" he asked in a hollow voice.

"Why would I chase you?" she said, surprised.

"Why, you ask?" he exclaimed, spreading out his arms like a king in a tragic opera. "Why? Because, it seems, I am a miserable human being, unworthy of compassion . . . I am useless. They're waiting for me to die. . ."

"Aha," Mrs. Syrovy thought calmly to herself.

The old man stepped close to his daughter and whispered secretively: "She chased me out of the house. 'Go,' she said, 'off with you . . . I've had you up to here.' "

"But why?"

"It's like this," the oldster said, and then he sat down heavily in a chair: "our maid left, supposedly to get married . . . And I said: If she wants to get married, let her go . . . There are plenty of maids in the world. I said: I'll go to an employment office and bring home a girl . . . But she said: You don't understand such things, I'll get a maid myself . . . All right, go then, if you're so smart . . . She brought home Katya. I didn't like her looks. I said: what kind of a maid is that, with a hairdo as high as a tower? I have a hunch that girl won't work out . . . Go away, she said, this is no business for a man. Fine . . . then on Saturday she started lighting the kitchen oven . . . I'm watching her . . . Katya, I said, is this any way to light an oven? Is this how they taught you to do it? And I showed her the right way. First you put in paper and wood shavings, and when that gets going you add a shovelful of coal. That's how you light an oven. But the way you do it is worthless . . . And she had the nerve to answer: If I had a husband like you, I'd pour boiling water on him . . . I was dumbfounded by her arrogance and told Mother. But she answered: Serves you right. A man's got no business in the kitchen . . . That's what she's like . . . She humiliates her own husband in front of a servant. . ."

"Stay with us for lunch, Daddy," said his daughter.

"Lunch? No . . . I don't care for charity . . . What kind of lunch do I need, anyway? Just give me some warm soup and a crust of dry bread to keep up my strength . . . Then I'll get up and go out into the world . . . When my own people chase me out, I'll find shelter with strangers . . . And I'll breathe my last in some far-off place, and nobody will even know about it . . . Yes, that's right. I've lived too long . . . I'm a burden to my own family. . ."

3 During lunch, however, Dad forgot that his troubled life was drawing to a close and that he was about to die under a stranger's roof. Eating put him in a better mood. After lunch he felt like gabbing. Incoherent thoughts floated to the threshold of his consciousness; he knitted his brows and began holding forth with a threatening mien:

"Did you know Sholar? . . . you didn't, because you were still too young . . . at that time you were still going to school . . . and this fellow Sholar made the statement . . . and I went with a whole deputation to the district director . . . How come, Mister Director, by what right do you exercise such extensive authority. . .? He was taken aback and said: You are familiar with the law? . . . Certainly, though I'm not a lawyer and I see right through these shenanigans . . . Then we had a meeting and I said: I am calling the meeting to order, but you choose your own chairman, I don't want to have anything more to do with it . . . For there is a certain person among you, and I will name him publicly if he doesn't come forward on his own . . . If he doesn't step up on his own I'll brand him an opportunist, but if he comes forward I won't use that word . . . The chairman said: These words were spoken publicly, whomever they apply to is to step forward . . . Sholar turned red and left the meeting and everyone saw that my accusation was correct . . . Yes, sir! . . . They all knew me, for I have always been a fighter . . . But you, as I see, still haven't got your stairs in order . . . it's a question of serious injury, I'll inform the public about it if there is no improvement . . . You go too far. . ."

"Take another piece of meat, Daddy," Mrs. Syrovy interrupted.

"I can't, dear daughter, I can't, you have no idea how weak I am . . . Last night I dreamed that I was in a big city, like Cologne on the Rhine . . . but it wasn't Cologne, there was a big barracks there like in Mlada Boleslav . . . and I was loading goods onto a wagon, shoelaces, nothing but shoelaces, there was no end to it and I was in an awful hurry . . . And nobody can explain to me what such a pile of shoelaces signifies . . . I felt a heavy pressure on my chest . . . Mother had a special belt made for me, lined with cat's fur . . . Cat's fur draws away all kinds of faintness, as has been demonstrated . . . But now I must go home, Mother is there alone, do you have a message for her? . . . You haven't visited us for a long time, that's not nice of you . . . Well, goodbye then, and visit us soon!"

4   As soon as the day turned cooler, the Syrovys went out for a walk. They strolled down the zig-zag village road winding its way through the valley. A hurdy-gurdy man stood on the little bridge over the stream and turned the handle of his instrument. Coatless old men sat on the wooden beams of the bridge. Dull thuds of falling bowling-pins resounded from garden restaurants.

The couple intended to turn aside into the fields, but their way was barred by a procession accompanied by blaring music. At its head marched a man dressed in the uniform of a bailiff; he had false mustaches and he rolled his eyes in an appalling way. Behind him rode several men and stocky women in folk costume; the manes of their horses were twisted into braids and decorated with streamers.

The garden restaurants were filled with city folk, looking forward to spending a pleasant Sunday afternoon under the colorful paper lanterns. Families camped under the widespread chestnut trees; the men sipped beer and chewed on their Virginia cigars; the women dunked rolls in their coffee cups; the children sucked red and yellow lemonades. Naked infants in baby carriages happily nibbled at their big toes. For the common citizen of Prague this was a perfect Sunday.

In the fields, the half-grown wheat was already waving to and fro. White butterflies fluttered phlegmatically over the blooming clover. A compost heap was crowned by wild poppies. The air smelled of fried beets.

The couple walked silently along the hedge, fighting the pesky flies that were attracted by perspiration.

The wife spoke at last: "I don't understand it, but I have a feeling that the landlord's wife has a grudge against me. The other day I greeted her and she didn't respond."

The clerk came to a halt: "That means trouble!" he exclaimed. "What have you done to her?"

"I don't know," the wife pondered, "but I think. . ."

"Well?"

"The other day, I think it was Wednesday, I couldn't open the window. She happened to pass by and I called to her: 'Mrs. Faktor, please, help me open the window. . .' But she only tossed her head, clenched her lips, and left . . . Could she have taken offense?"

"Why would she take offense? After all, nothing happened . . . Perhaps it's some sort of misunderstanding . . . But I beg you, be careful . . . No ill will. We are little people. We are subject to landlords and have to do their bidding . . . The best thing is to stay low and avoid problems . . . Good will and calm. You have to give the landlord's wife her due. We can't afford to be proud, my salary is too low for that. . ."

"Don't worry, everything is all right . . . But surely you don't want me to say 'please accept my sincerest compliments' to her?"

"No, certainly not . . . I won't stand for any fawning. I want to be an equal among equals . . . You are the wife of a government employee and you needn't put up with any impertinence. . ."

Chapter Sixteen

1   The darkness in the street is congealing. A group of youths is gathered under the glowing streetlamp at the corner; fragments of conversation float up to the clerk, who is leaning on the windowsill.

". . . he said, forget it, show us a ticket or get the hell out of here. . ."

". . . they shifted him to right wing and he still wasn't worth a damn. . ."

". . . I hate to say it, but they were really hot. . ."

". . . you tried, I know, but I just couldn't shake the guy covering me. . ."

". . . there's too much dribbling, you've got to pass the ball.."

"I couldn't stand to see you screwing up like that," said a hunchbacked youth, and he squirted a spray of spit through his teeth.

"Easy for you to say," a gangly fellow answered, "but that was some cannonball shot, let me tell you. . ."

". . . Hey, there goes Blanka. . ."

Hurrying across the street was a girl with her nose in the air.

"Come and join us, your highness, our eyes are hungry for a feast," the hunchback called to her.

"Look," the girl said, waving her hand contemptuously. "Count me out!"

"Certainly, certainly," the hunchback made an ironic bow, "give my regards to your parents. . ."

The girl said something that could no longer be heard. The hunchback answered with a cynical insult.

"What sort of people are they. . ." the clerk shuddered. "I can't even understand their language. Lucky we live in a policeman's house . . . Such people would kill you as soon as look at you. Now they're whispering among themselves; doubtless they're discussing some knavery. I will have to bring them to the policeman's attention. They should all be locked up to keep them from making trouble."

Stepping away from the window, he could still overhear a child's voice:

"Mr. Fara, Dad would like to borrow a detective novel."

"My compliments to your dad," wheezed a male bass, "and tell him to first return the razor he borrowed from me. . ."

The clerk closed the window and went to bed.

2   Meanwhile, dim figures were slinking up the path to the policeman's house. The teacher Soltys stood in front of the door to his apartment and greeted each newcomer with a whispered: "God be with you."

The dim light of a lamp lit up their faces. They were old men in long-tailed black coats and grandmotherly women wrapped in old-fashioned scarves.

The clock on the school building was just striking eleven when a peculiar, choked voice could be heard from the ground floor. It sounded as if someone was desperately moaning for help.

The clerk sat up in bed and with eyes wide open and filled with anguish, he stared into the darkness.

"You hear?" he whispered, terror-stricken.

His wife had been half asleep. "What's going on?" she asked sleepily.

"Down there . . . down below. . ." the clerk gibbered, "they're strangling somebody. . ."

"Shh!" his wife said, and she put her hand on his shoulder. They both listened intently.

In a while they again heard moaning sounds, which seemed to come from the throat of a woman stricken by inhuman pain. Then they could make out individual words.

". . . I shall repent, for I behold the church," the voice wailed, "I shall repent, for I behold the people . . . They called but they were not heard . . . and there arose great confusion, and the sinner could not be distinguished from the righteous . . . many came but few were saved . . . the Lord conceived great anger at the people of Babylon, for they sowed the seed of iniquity . . . Alas, alas . . . he is coming, I feel him coming . . . welcome, brother, and pronounce the saving word. . ."

"Who is coming?" whispered the clerk, trembling all over. "What's all this noise? Good God, what's going on? Go downstairs and see what's going on."

"I know now," his wife answered calmly: "those are the spiritualists who meet at the Soltyses. They have a revolving board and they summon up spirits. Mrs. Soltys asked me to join them, but I told them I don't believe in those things."

"Is this permissible, calling up spirits in the middle of the night?" the clerk complained. He felt better and began to grumble: "We sank a lot of bloodmoney into this house and now we can't even have a decent night's rest. You can summon all the spirits you like before ten o'clock. But after ten there's supposed to be peace and quiet, and all performances are forbidden. I won't just let it go . . . I'll take it up with the landlord. . ."

"Come on, relax," his wife said soothingly, "Mr. Soltys is such a nice man, so courteous and obliging. There are far worse tenants than that. In our old house, there were brawls downstairs in the tavern every night. The drunkards even tore out the stairway railing . . . Every place has its drawbacks and you've got to put up with them. Every one has a hobby. Some people occupy themselves with spirits, you collect foreign stamps. . ."

"Stamp-collecting doesn't bother anybody," answered the clerk; "it's a quiet activity. But disturbances can't be tolerated in an orderly house. Besides, let me tell you, summoning spirits is against the law. . ."

"Go to sleep now," his wife said soothingly.

"Sleep. . ." the clerk grumbled, "how can I sleep? I'm all shaken up. . ."

3 It was a bright morning and the policeman was contemplating the way his alfalfa was growing on the gentle slope that separated the vegetable garden from the flower beds. Mrs. Syrovy came out into the yard to dump her refuse on the garbage heap.

"Up so early?" he called to her in a friendly tone; but inside he was thinking: "I don't look and yet I see everything. I don't even have to look. So you dump garbage in my yard, do you?"

Aloud, he continued: "I'm taking a look at the alfalfa. It looks poor."

Mrs. Syrovy said: "Do you think it will survive?"

"I figure it will," the policeman answered, "because the moon is waxing." He himself was smiling like the moon.

But inside he was angered not only by the dumping of garbage in his yard, but also by the urge he felt to smile at his tenant. He shot a sharp glance at Mrs. Syrovy and declared to himself: "Anybody who doesn't know me might get the wrong idea . . . But they'd better not think that way, or they'll be in deep trouble. I can be a mean dog! You think I'm here to clean up your garbage, do you? Am I your servant or your landlord? Answer me. . .!"

"And how did the lady sleep last night?" he asked sweetly.

"Badly," Mrs. Syrovy answered; "we had a restless night."

The policeman raised his head. "Restless?" he asked suspiciously. "Can there be anything in my house that would disturb your rest? Who disturbed you? I'll bet the news dealer invited his gang and played cards all night. I'll put a stop to that. I'll show him. He gives me a measly seven thousand as a down payment and twelve hundred in rent and he thinks he's got a right to make noise . . . I've had my eye on him for some time. During the week he wears a wooden leg, but on Sundays and holidays he's got to sport a rubber prosthesis, the dandy! Such a show-off! If he paid decent rent, let him buy ten rubber legs! . . . I'll have to put my foot down. . ."

"Oh no," Mrs. Syrovy interjected, "there was no problem with the news dealer. It was the Soltyses who raised a rumpus. We couldn't even sleep. . ."

"Is that so?" said the landlord. "Our teacher? So there you have it! That's where education gets you. And he seemed so peaceful . . . quiet as a mouse . . . But I saw right through him. He explains to me about the stars as if I was just a dumb oaf who never heard of stars . . . 'If we consider that a light ray takes hundreds of thousands of years before it completes its journey, our insignificance makes us tremble.' I understand your insinuations. You are insignificant, but I am not insignificant. A down payment of fifteen thousand — these days that means nothing. Give me twenty thousand, then you can prattle about stars all you like. Don't think you can lord it over me with your education. I never had much schooling, but I have a good head on my shoulders."

The policeman went on in this vein. His face flushed and he got angrier and angrier, for he felt the need to rouse himself against a presumed wrong. He belonged to that prevalent type of domineering people who enjoy feeling insulted.

"We're already lying in bed," Mrs. Syrovy continued in a calm voice, "our eyes about to close . . . Then suddenly we hear a terrible commotion. My husband jumps up: what's going on?"

"And what was the cause of all the noise?" the policeman inquired.

"They were summoning up spirits. My husband said: 'I have no objection to summoning spirits. But I must insist that it take place quietly. I am tired and need my rest.' Those people didn't leave till late at night. We couldn't fall asleep for hours. I said we would have to inform the landlord, to put an end to such disturbances."

"You can rest assured that I'll put an end to it," said the policeman, "for I don't tolerate spirits in my house. That's all we need . . . In my house there's got to be peace and order. I didn't build a habitation for spirits."

4   The policeman left Mrs. Syrovy and with a determined mien entered the ground-floor apartment. Mr. Soltys was sitting at a table, immersed in a book. His wife was busily sewing. The canary washopping around in its cage, lustily piping to drown out the whir of the sewing machine.

The policeman said good morning.

"The Lord be with you," the teacher replied in a muffled voice. "What can we do for our landlord?"

"Actually. . ." the policeman began, running his finger around his shirt-collar, "actually a major complaint has been lodged against you, if I may put it that way. . ." He was at a loss for words and started rubbing his hands, smiling fulsomely.

"You don't say," said the surprised Mr. Soltys.

"Yes, it's true. . ." the policeman continued, tenaciously searching for words: "They said: 'There was an awful uproar in the house,' and I said: 'That must be looked into.' Easy does it, that's my motto. Consideration for the other fellow; that's the way. . ."

"I don't understand you," said the teacher softly.

"There is nothing to understand," the policeman flared up. "I am not the kind of person to stand in anyone's way. But Mrs. Syrovy complains that you summon spirits. She says it interferes with their sleep. I don't put much trust in her words. I know who I'm dealing with. Those are people who think everybody else is dirt and look down their noses at everybody. I've had my eye on them for quite a while and I am beginning to lose my patience with them. Still, I've got to tell you that I don't tolerate spirits in the house. Summoning up spirits is against house rules, because it involves noise."

"But my dear landlord," the teacher objected in a heartfelt tone, "I understand what you mean, but. . ."

"Look here," the policeman interrupted. "After ten o'clock all kinds of performances are forbidden. That's the rule in the entire world. There will be no more summoning of spirits, and that's that!"

"Look here, sir," the teacher said plaintively. "I have to keep in contact with spirits. . ."

"For God's sake," the policeman retorted rudely, "what profit is there in that? I certainly don't believe in spirits."

"It's true that some people feel no need to make contact with the Unknown . . . But a person has other needs besides bodily appetites. Even if you look at the matter from a practical viewpoint: Grandpa Hynek, who appeared at one of our seances, recommended that we rent an apartment from you . . . I never listened to anyone else's advice. For Grandpa Hynek, while still alive always excelled thanks to his rare wisdom, and I've always benefited when I followed his counsel. If it hadn't been for his wise words, I would have looked for a different place to live. . ."

"Ha, ha, that man really saved my skin, good old Grandpa Hynek," sneered the policeman. "What the devil do you think, mister? Do you think I couldn't have found another tenant? My Lord, these days you can get tenants by the carload. Sure, I was saved by Grandpa Hynek. You gave me fifteen thousand down and you're paying three thousand a year in rent. And for that I should put up with spirits marching around my house? Where would that get me? And furthermore, let me warn you that spiritualism is against the law . . . This could mean trouble for me in the department, because a policeman is supposed to suppress illegal activities, not support them. That's how it is, mister . . . In short: I won't tolerate spirits in my house and that's that!"

The teacher rose to his feet and gently put his hand on the policeman's shoulder.

"Landlord," he said softly, "you implied that the rent we are paying is low. In terms of our income, at least, it is a sizeable amount . . . It isn't easy for us, believe me . . . But never mind . . . However, as far as contacts with our brothers are concerned, my wife and I cannot forego that. After all, that's the only thing that lifts a person from the dust of the commonplace up to the starry heights. We don't weep over the loss of our loved ones, because we know that they continue to live and share all our joys and sorrows. . ."

"That's all well and good," the policeman said harshly, "but it isn't permitted, and that's my last word. . ."

"I have not yet finished, landlord," the teacher said softly; "there is still the matter of the rent. If you were to permit our seances, we might be willing to add a bit to our rent."

The policeman perked up his ears.

"Go on, teacher," he said in a kindlier tone; "I will accommodate you as best I can. You know me, you know that I have a soft spot for tenants. Anyone who approaches me the right way can twist me around his finger. . ."

"I'm willing to raise the rent by five hundred crowns a year," the teacher continued.

"Five hundred? What an idea! Don't forget that this involves illegal activity! Let's say a thousand, that's more like it!"

"Eight hundred."

"Fine," the policeman agreed, "just to show you the kind of person I am. I don't want anyone to think that I stand in the way of communicating with the dear departed. Nobody can prevent you from doing that; I'll back you up. Anyone who wrongs you will have to settle with me. Eight hundred. It's a deal. And I will stop Mrs. Syrovy from any further incitement. . ."

He left, shaking his head in wonder.

"Who would have thought," he pondered, "that there's profit even in spirits. And nice profit, a big profit! Eight hundred . . . That's good. It will lower our debt to the bank."

He hurried to tell his wife the good news.

Chapter Seventeen

1   This was the day the policemen had off. He finished some heavy tasks in the garden and now, in khaki pants without a jacket, he strolled along the paths, which he had carefully strewn with fine, blue gravel.

It was the end of June, and the days were ripening into a sweltering summer. The landlord inspected his handiwork and was pleased to see that the garden was profitably thriving. The kohlrabi was growing massive, spreading its broad leaves; leeks covered their beds with succulent stalks; voluminous heads of lettuce rested in their leafy, violet-tinged nests. Pink and blue violets exhaled a faint aroma, reminiscent of the smell of French facepowder. The policeman circled the beds, bending down now and again to pull out weeds that deprived nobler plants of nourishment. Then he sat down on a bench and gazed with dreamy eyes at the red roof of his house, where pigeons puffed up their throats and sweetly cooed. The policeman's heart was flooded with tenderness, and this is the way he talked to himself: "This house with that beautiful red roof is mine, and so are the pigeons. They've gotten used to the attic after two weeks of imprisonment; they won't fly away any longer, for they know very well that they are my property." And he envied the pigeons for being able to circle in the air and look at his property from on high. "I know my house from all sides," he mused, "but how does it look from above? Surely it's beautiful that way, too, more beautiful than the other houses."

He got up and went into the yard, filled with rows of rabbit hutches and chicken coops. As soon as the rabbits saw the policeman, they squatted on their haunches and placed their front paws on the wire screen, begging for food. The landlord handed them dandelion leaves and watched with amusement how they fought over them and hungrily dispatched them, their noses going through comic contortions.

"Eat, eat, you foolish fuzzballs," he muttered; "get fat in a hurry, I want to see you soon on a skillet. You have no idea how good you taste in a cream sauce."

He then turned to the chicken coops and said: "And you, my little hens, I will let you out. Look for worms, but stay out of the garden; all you'd do is cause damage. You are allowed to scratch for worms in the tenants' beds; the tenants are not allowed to harm you. But stay off the neighbor's property, unless you're very careful. The neighbor is a ruffian and might harm you. And keep laying eggs with diligence. In the summer eggs are cheap, but in winter they sell for a crown apiece. One crown added to another crown makes two crowns. Crowns stick together, and soon there is a pile of them. That's how it adds up. . ."

"Quiet, Amina, sit!" he shouted at the dog, who was tugging at her chain, begging for a bit of attention. "That's all right, yes, I know . . . good dog, good . . . Keep a sharp watch, don't let bad people harm your master's property."

He stroked the dog, who went mad with joy, turned over on her back, and waved all four legs in the air.

"I am now going to the cellar for my tools," said the policeman. "I have to fix the stairs, right, Amina?"

Amina stretched herself and whimpered, for her heart was overflowing with tempestuous emotions.

2 The landlord had hardly left when the neighbor's dog appeared. He had been making a big show of courting Amina.

He was a surly animal, with rough yellowish fur and a white cataract in his left eye; yet in spite of this lack of charms, Amina greeted him courteously, for he helped to shorten her boring hours on the chain. The yellow dog was happy to see his ladyfriend alone, and hoped that the time had come for reciprocation of his advances. He began to jump around Amina and nip at her ears while emitting short, eager barks. He launched into the rites which are part of canine courtship.

However, the policeman suddenly returned to the yard from the cellar, and seeing the strange dog he stamped his feet angrily.

"Scat, you tailor's mutt!" the policeman shouted, rolling his eyes.

"That's all I need, to have other people's dogs running around my property!"

The yellow dog was frightened. He jumped over the fence, accompanied by the policeman's imprecations and the furious barking of Amina, who gathered that her master did not approve of the liaison and changed her affection into hate.

"I told you," Amina barked: "my master doesn't wish me to associate with you. Leave me alone, you ugly brute, we don't want you here. . ."

The tailor's dog, feeling safe behind the fence, turned his snout sideways and let go a furious howl to express his disappointment over jilted love.

"Nice goings on. . ." grumbled the policeman; "we don't need any puppies . . . What good are puppies? Nobody will take them. There's no profit in it. I'll tell the tailor that he'd better tie up his dog, if he doesn't want me to give him what for."

He ground his teeth and waved his fist at his neighbor's house.

3   In the afternoon Mr. Syrovy had visitors. It was his niece, a corpulent, ruddy-faced woman, and her two children. Breathing heavily, she complained that the stairs were too steep and that climbing the hill had caused her heart to pound.

Mrs. Syrovy gave the children some candy and asked them to play outside on the terrace. The curly six-year-old boy and red-headed, pink little girl went out the door holding hands.

The corpulent woman sipped her coffee and chatted. Her conversation was so monotonous that it made her listeners sleepy. The clerk felt his eyes closing; he excused himself and left for the bedroom.

"You have a nice place," said the ruddy-faced woman, sighing; "there is green all around and healthy air. Only it's a bit far. And how do you get along with the landlord?"

"Very well," answered Mrs. Syrovy; "he is obliging and takes care of all our requests. We're satisfied with him."

"Be glad," the niece said; "nowadays that's very rare."

She paused, and then added: "And your coffee is good. How much do you pay for it?"

"Seven crowns for an eighth of a kilo," said Mrs. Syrovy.

"Just like in town," the ruddy-faced woman sighed; "it's

the same everywhere . . . So your landlord is decent? That's good, that's good . . . We're not that lucky. Ours is trying to get rid of us. He says: 'You're living here scot-free. And I can't afford that.' Some merchant offered a lot of money for our apartment. The landlord tried to get the housing court to evict us. But the court decided that we don't have to move out. And where could we move? We have no money, so we've got to stay where we are. Now every day the handle of our door is smeared with excrement. I know who's responsible. It's the super's handiwork. But we haven't been able to catch him in the act. We're trying, but we can't get any justice anywhere. . ."

"You have it rough," Mrs. Syrovy said with compassion.

4   The children were attracted by the sandpile in front of the house. They began to pick out blue and rosy stones, mumbling pensively to themselves.

"It's a pretty little house, isn't it?" the red-headed girl said with great delight.

"It is not a pretty little house," the boy stubbornly insisted.

"It is a gor-geous little house," the girl drew out the words in a sing-song voice.

"Ours is prettier," the boy maintained. "In our house we have mirrors on the stairway."

"Yeaah," the girl agreed.

"We have a red carpet on the stairs."

"Yeaah."

"And painted roses on the walls."

"Yeaah."

"And the superintendent has a jackdaw that sits on his shoulder — whee, birdie!"

"Yeaah."

The policeman stealthily approached from behind and listened to the children's talk.

"And this house has no mirrors or painted roses," the boy continued, contemptuously wrinkling his forehead. "It's ugly, ugly, the ugliest of all."

The policeman flushed with anger. "They are slandering my house," he rasped; "how dare they!"

"What are you doing here?" he shouted roughly.

The children were startled.

"Whose are you?" the policeman pressed on.

The children didn't say a word.

"Don't you know how to talk? How long am I supposed to wait for an answer?"

Seeing that the children were on the verge of tears, the policeman decided to adopt a milder tone. "Otherwise I won't learn anything from them," he decided.

"Whoever told you that my house is ugly?" the policeman said in a pleasant voice. "I'll bet it was Mrs. Syrovy, wasn't it?"

"Go on, children, tell me and I'll show you some rabbits," the policeman cajoled. "Or was it Mr. Syrovy who said it?"

But he waited in vain for an answer. He turned red, stamped his feet, and hissed: "Scat, you urchins, or I'll whack you with a stick!"

At that moment Mrs. Syrovy appeared on the terrace with her niece. The policeman stopped, shifted his cap, and said: "I was just watching how nicely the children play together . . . Sand — that's what they love. I know. Go on, play, my little ones, and don't look at me that way. I won't hurt you — never! I'm good with children."

"You have exhilarating air here," chirped the ruddy-faced woman. "And what a beautiful view," she added, gazing at the city spread out at her feet, a smoky, bluish, enormous city with its cupolas and towers.

"That's true," the policeman said proudly; "our air is like mountain air . . . I certainly picked out a good spot for my house."

Mrs. Syrovy called the children for their afternoon snack.

The policeman glanced gloomily at the spot where a moment earlier the children had been standing, and growled: "Healthy air, she says . . . I'll give you healthy air! Healthy air and a beautiful view are only for those who pay their rent . . . And not for any old bag that wanders in . . . And I won't stand for visitors in my house. What kind of business is that? Should I allow outsiders to wander around here without my knowledge? They might cause damage. . ."

He went to the garden, where he stopped in front of an apple sapling. The sole pink blossom had faded, leaving behind a green fruit glistening in the rays of the sun.

"Here an apple is growing," the policeman said to himself, "the first apple from my garden . . . I have to watch them carefully. Heaven help anyone who touches them. I'll brrrreak their paws. . .! The garden will be locked up and nobody will be allowed admittance, especially children. Children are worse than cattle!"

Chapter Eighteen

1   When the policeman returned home, he said to his wife: "Anastazie, at the Syrovys they slander our house. They don't like it. They're saying that other places have mirrors in the halls and rugs on the stairs. They kept needling me. Our house isn't beautiful enough for them. And soft-hearted as I am, I kept quiet and swallowed my anger. That's the reward I get."

"Is that so!" his wife said angrily. She picked up the enameled milk jug and went off to the grocer's.

After she left, the policeman turned to his children.

"Drop everything and go outside. Walk around and listen to what people are saying. And if anybody says anything about us, come and tell me right away."

The little girl jumped up and nimbly ran outside. The youth ambled out the door, went into the street, and sat down listlessly on a pile of gravel. He pulled a pen-knife out of his pocket and began whittling on a piece of wood, sticking out the tip of his tongue.

The policeman's wife entered the grocery store, which is where the neighborhood women tended to gather at nightfall. In the back of the grocery there was a laundry room with a mechanical wringer. Here women engaged in heated discussions, collecting and distributing news from the entire quarter. There wasn't a single man or woman whose personal affairs were not flushed out in the laundry room. For it was difficult to conceal household matters in a neighborhood such as this, which had only recently become attached to the growing metropolis and still had a small-town character.

The policeman's wife enjoyed a high rank in the grocery, based on her husband's official status. A policeman's power among humble people is limitless, for a policeman bears with him a piece of the state's legal might. He is a privileged person and the law protects him more than it does an ordinary citizen.

"The Syrovys had a visit today," recounted the policeman's wife. "A woman came with her two children."

"Is that so?" said the grocer, busily arranging chicory on the shelf, trying to create symmetrical designs out of the multicolored packages.

"Yes," the woman continued, "but her visitors were nothing to boast about. My husband said: 'She had such a raucous voice that her screeching could be heard through the whole house.' "

The grocer let out a grunt that could be interpreted as agreement.

"My husband knows that woman . . . Oh, she's a real number!" The policeman's wife lowered her voice to a whisper: "Before the war, she ran a whorehouse in Jewtown. One time, my husband had to restore order when her guests got into a fracas."

The grocer cleared his throat and said: "People often say something that leads to trouble."

"Just imagine: they don't like our house . . . They compared it to an old dump; they said the walls are cracking and the ceiling might drop on somebody's head. . ."

At that moment the grocer's wife entered the store, and on hearing the last words she asked: "Who could say such a thing?"

Her husband winked at her furiously and said: "What

are you doing in the shop? I'll handle the customers. Go chop some wood, we ran out of firewood."

"Anyone who doesn't like our house is free to leave," the policeman's wife continued. "Who needs them? My husband said that a doctor was interested in that apartment. Those people are so conceited, they wanted to raise a peacock, even though they live from hand to mouth. But Faktor didn't allow it. He said: 'Forget the peacock, it's up to me to decide which animals can be kept and which cannot.' I think she expects that I'm going to bow to her, but she'll have to wait a long time before that happens. Am I the landlady or is she the landlady? What do you say to that, Mr. Mejstrik?"

The grocer merely answered: "Oh well, now, sure," and bent down over a crate of cabbage.

"I've got to go now," declared the policeman's wife. "Put that half-pound of sugar on the cuff. We'll pay after Sunday."

"There's no hurry," said the grocer obligingly.

After she left, the grocer shouted toward the kitchen: "How many times must I tell you, Majdalena, not to talk in front of the policeman's wife? Keep quiet or there'll be trouble. I prefer to keep out of it. I don't want to have any quarrel with the policeman. Policemen are never in the wrong."

"But I didn't say anything," Majdalena objected.

"It's not just a matter of not saying anything," the grocer instructed; "you have to make yourself small, so that you can't even be seen. They can do a lot of harm."

2   Next, the policeman's wife approached a group of women sitting on the porch in front of the door and announced that Mecl the tailor was a louse, because he threw a clod at the policeman's hen, which had strayed into his garden. She said that the whole street would soon learn what happens to people who don't respect private property. The policeman would see to that. The women received the announcement of this dispute between neighbors with gratification. News of the impending showdown flew through the streets and reached the ears of every inhabitant.

The policeman walked into his garden, watering can in hand. At that moment the tailor came out, attached a hose to the faucet, and got ready to water his flowerbeds. The people from across the street gathered in front of their doors, eager to follow the course of events.

The two antagonists greeted each other with cool dignity.

"Will you be watering?" asked the policeman.

"That's right," the tailor answered. "There's no sign of rain."

"No, not a sign."

"The lettuce is looking good," said the tailor, feeling edgy about the upcoming conflict.

"But the celery isn't worth much," answered the policeman, knitting his brows.

They began like a person sitting down before a plate of plums. He first picks out the ripe, juicy ones, contemptuous of wrinkled, spoiled fruit. But appetite grows with eating, and after polishing off the healthy plums he gladly takes the slightly rotten ones, too. And he ends up eating everything.

The two neighbors proceeded the same way. At first they chose their words carefully, adding a friendly smile.

119

After having exhausted the supply of polite expressions, they moved on to vague innuendos.

The policeman mentioned his hen. The tailor countered with the remark that he didn't lavish care on his garden to let somebody's vile birds dig it up. The policeman replied that chickens lack reason; the tailor, on the other hand, is endowed with reason and therefore should judge the hen's transgression in a reasonable manner. The tailor responded that this was precisely the reason why the policeman should make sure that his fowl did not transgress the bounds of his property. The policeman replied that there was no way to keep watch over hens; a hen lacks the intelligence to respect private property. The tailor hinted that the policeman deliberately incited the hens to damage his garden.

"We know all about it," said the tailor, winking.

"A fat lot you know," answered the policeman. "Look who's talking."

"You've got no business in my garden," the tailor said firmly.

"You're not worth bothering with!" the policeman shouted.

The two men began to trade insults as if tossing a dead cat back and forth over a wall.

The tailor was winning, for he had a nimbler tongue. He accused the policeman of oppressing his parents; just the other day the tailor gave the policeman's mother a cup of coffee because he was so touched by her poverty. Before you shoot off your mouth, the tailor advised, see to it that your parents don't need the charity of strangers. It's ridiculous to play the big landlord and starve your own relatives.

"You. . . you. . ." the policeman screamed, "you show-offs . . . You don't impress me with your balconies and swings . . . I've outgrown things like that long ago . . .

120

Some people have balconies and play at gentry and in the meantime their daughter. . ."

"What's that about my daughter?" the tailor exclaimed belligerently.

The policeman suddenly stopped short, for he remembered legal liability and his own official position. He merely mumbled that he knew quite a few things which he'd rather not talk about .

"I don't stick my nose into other people's business," he said.

"I should hope not," answered the tailor, and he left with a feeling of victory.

The crowd of onlookers dispersed, disappointed. The grocer spotted his wife among the women and called out to her: "Majdalena, go home! The milk is running over!"

When she came back to the store, he said angrily: "Why do you listen to this nonsense, you old gossip? Haven't I told you not to get mixed up in anything!"

"Mixed up? What are you talking about?" the wife defended herself. "I don't even listen. I don't pay attention and I don't even know what's going on."

"When there is a quarrel somewhere, you stay out of it. We have no business getting involved in it. We are tradespeople. The tailor buys from us. Who knows, it could go to court and you'll be called as a witness. I am not going to offend any customers. If anything were to happen, you simply say that you're as deaf as a board and don't know anything about anything. Understand?"

3   After the tailor's departure, the policeman felt dark dissatisfaction about the outcome of the contest. He was afraid the audience may have gotten the impression that the tailor had triumphed, which would diminish his reputation throughout the neighborhood.

Tormented by doubts, he knocked on Mrs. Syrovy's door and asked her whether she had heard the tailor calling him a 'scoundrel.'

"He dared to insult me," he said, "as you doubtless heard. He committed a grave transgression, for insults of the police are punishable by imprisonment."

"I didn't hear a thing," Mrs. Syrovy answered, "because I was pounding cutlets . . . I know there was some sort of disturbance, but as to what actually happened, that I know nothing about."

"But surely," the policeman insisted, "you must have heard the word 'scoundrel.' After all, he was yelling so hard it must have been heard far and wide."

"I may be wrong, but it seems to me that he wouldn't dare to insult you," said Mrs. Syrovy. "He must surely realize the trouble it might get him into, and he's not going to bring disaster down on his head. I only heard some talk about a hen. That's all I know, and I can't say any more."

"But even if you didn't hear his exact words," the policeman pressed on, "you'll certainly admit that a person like that is capable of any insult. Why, he's a miscreant, capable of anything. But I warn him not to play games with me; or I'll see to it that he rots in jail. I carry a lot of weight in high places. It won't help him one bit that he owns a house with a balcony . . . But I'm surprised you didn't hear him call me names; and I'm sorry you're taking this attitude."

"I tell what I know, and I don't what I don't."

"All right, all right. . ." said the policeman, with a bitter smile. "Now at least I know . . . I never thought you'd let your landlord down. At least now I know where I stand."

4   When the clerk came home from the office and sat down to dinner, his wife told him about the landlord's quarrel with the neighbor. The clerk listened with a worried face, slowly nodding his head.

"Mecl the tailor," he said, "is a disorderly and quarrelsome person. He doesn't try to be on good terms with his neighbors. And I would guess that he can be quite malicious. I know that he throws pieces of glass and all sorts of waste over the fence, polluting our garden. If it wasn't for the policeman's patience, quarrels would break out every day."

He bent over his plate and began to slice the cutlet with a serious expression on his face.

"To live in peace and quiet with the rest of mankind," he declared, brandishing his knife for emphasis, "is a precondition of successful existence. Let Mecl the tailor keep that in mind. We, thank God, can truthfully say that we get along with everyone. And that's why we deservedly enjoy popularity. Well, I've eaten my fill, so now, dear, give me some black coffee."

His wife put a cup of black coffee on the table and said: "The landlord wanted me to confirm that the tailor had insulted him."

"And what did you tell him?" the clerk asked nervously.

"That I didn't hear anything."

"You said the right thing, my good wife. Don't listen to anything and don't pry into anything. It's not a good idea to get involved in other people's quarrels. We want to get along with everyone. And for that reason we must be deaf and blind."

"However," the wife said, "the landlord's children stopped greeting me some time ago. That seems strange."

"Stopped greeting you?" the clerk pondered. "So be it. They apparently don't have any manners. Their education has been neglected. Ignore it and go your own way; be clever like me."

He sighed. "I worked hard in the office today. The chief got sick and now everything's on my shoulders. I have to rest. Yes, that's it . . . I'll indulge myself with a little breather. . ."

Chapter Nineteen

1   It was unbearably hot for several days in a row. The air stood as motionless as a pillar; plants and trees were covered with rusty dust. The streets blazed like a brick oven; people crept along, hugging the walls of houses. Winged pods spiraled down from the maple trees that lined the tortuous paths. Geese rested along the hedges, with one leg nestled under a wing and the head melancholically tilted to the side. The policeman's hens gave up their restless running and settled down in the shallow pits they'd dug by the side of the ditch; there they sat in rigid immobility, their eyes covered by a bluish membrane. Her snout resting on her paws, Amina lay in front of her doghouse, lost in dreams and hardly aware of the flies that circled her pus-filled eyelids.

In the afternoon, a pudgy, yellow-bordered cloud

appeared in the sky, which was blue as tempered steel. Suddenly there was movement. The trees rustled and a whirl of dust rose in the road, snatching up pieces of paper and bits of straw. From the fields came a wave of coolness. The sky grew dark with a sinister gray, and the sound of a storm boomed from the distance. Amid noisy shouting, the women began to close windows and take laundry off the lines. Old men lifted their worried faces to the sky and warned: "Something big is coming."

A zigzag bolt of lightning split the sky, accompanied by a dry rumble that sounded like the ripping of a stout piece of cloth. The storm rolled with thunder, and torrents of water streamed down to earth.

2   After the storm passed, grumbling darkly and irritably as it receded and transforming its might into a fine drizzle, the Syrovys' kitchen filled with smoke. Unable to penetrate to the outside through the damp air, it pushed its way back through the oven door. They had to call the oven man, the policeman's brother-in-law.

He gloomily inspected the oven and said: "It's not just the storm. It needs a better draught." He laid out his tools and set to work. Silently he took the tiles apart, kneaded sticky putty, and chiseled bricks into shape, melancholically working away amid clouds of soot. By noon he had finished; he filled the oven with wood-shavings and lit some paper. At first, the flame timidly licked the wood, as if trying out its taste; then it roared with full force. Soon the stove was aglow.

The laconic man wiped his nose with the back of his hand and declared: "It's all fixed now. I think the stove's in good shape now. But if you have any trouble, call me by all means and I'll fix it for you. But I don't think that will be necessary."

He shifted his feet, scratched the back of his head, and added, looking gloomily at the ground: "I'm walking around in my last pair of shoes. And my clothes are full of holes. That's how it is."

He lifted his eyes toward Mrs. Syrovy, who looked at him without understanding.

"I said," he continued, "that my clothes are in rags. An awful life. Would you by any chance have an old suit that your husband wants to get rid of?"

Mrs. Syrovy understood at last, and sprang to life with the fire of generosity. She went into the hall, and took out of the closet the suit with polka-dots the color of a trout's back.

"How about this one?" she asked the oven man.

The laconic man picked up the suit, stepped up to the window, and inspected it from all sides, testing with his hand the quality of the cloth. Quiet joy glistened in his teary eyes.

"The Lord bless you, madam," he whispered gratefully, "a great suit, top-grade material. I'll walk around like a lord. My wife will be proud."

"Wear it out in good health," said Mrs. Syrovy.

3   While they were talking together and the laconic man was loudly expressing the pleasure he felt concerning the suit he'd been donated, the landlady scurried up to the first floor like a weasel and burst into the news dealer's apartment.

She said: "I've got to hear what those two down there are talking about."

She positioned herself near the half-open door and listened with a rapt expression. From down below she heard the oven man's voice, as he praised the quality of the cloth and promised to perform any needed service in return for the gift.

"What did my brother-in-law want from them?" the landlady asked eagerly.

"I really don't know," said the news dealer's wife. "Maybe he came to fix their oven."

"And what kind of suit is he talking about?" the landlady inquired.

"He got Mr. Syrovy's old suit."

"He got a suit? Fine goings on. And he didn't tell us a thing about it. He's always reaching for a hand-out. He has big eyes, our brother. Whatever he sees, he's got to have . . . My husband's going to have a fit when he finds out his brother is in cahoots with the tenants. That's the gratitude we get. . ."

She waved her arm, ran downstairs, and rushed into the street.

4   In the evening, when the policeman went off duty, his wife informed him that his brother was deceitful. Without a word, the policeman put on his jacket and went to see the laconic man.

"What did you do at the Syrovys, Alois?" he inquired.

"What would I be doing? The oven was out of kilter," answered the oven man. "So I fixed it. . ."

"Hm. . . And what did you get from Mrs. Syrovy?"

"What is there to get? I didn't get anything. . ."

"Don't you deny it!" the policeman bellowed. "You got something, no doubt about it! Nothing escapes me, you should know that by now . . . I'm a pretty clever fellow. You got a suit. Show me!"

"What suit. . .?" the oven man said evasively.

"Don't worry, you fool," the policeman pressed on, "I

won't take it away from you. I don't care about your old rags. . ."

The laconic man let himself be persuaded and showed the policeman the gift.

The policeman deftly opened the jacket, examined the lining, felt the pockets, and then said in an indifferent tone: "Well . . . to tell you the truth, it isn't worth a lot. You're not going to impress anybody with that outfit . . . But since I'm in a generous mood, I'll give you a fiver for it. . ."

"No, sir," the oven man insisted, lovingly stroking the material, "this is a very special piece of clothing and I am glad to have it. . ."

"You're nothing but a pumpkin-head," the policeman said sternly, "you're so proud of this junk, and you don't see it's as porous as a sieve. The wind will blow right through the pants. My boy is starting an apprenticeship, and I would have this suit altered for him so he can wear it out behind the counter. Like I said, I'll give you a fiver. Take it as long as I'm in this mood. . ."

"What good is a fiver to me?" countered the in-law. "I glance at it and it's gone. But the suit will be useful for a long time, it's made of lasting material. . ."

"I'm amazed you're so fond of it," the policeman said in an insinuating tone; "you won't even be able to wear it. You are tall and skinny, and Syrovy is like a stunted sparrow."

The oven man thought it over and measured the length of the trousers against his legs. Indeed, they only reached down to the middle of his calves.

Nevertheless, he had become fond of the suit and decided not to part with it.

"I'm not selling," he said firmly.

The policeman's eyes flashed angrily. "You won't sell,"

Chapter Twenty

1   The next day was a holiday. Mrs. Syrovy stayed home after dinner, but the clerk decided to visit his Uncle Krystof.

"I haven't seen him for a long time," he said, "and it isn't right to neglect relatives."

"Go ahead," his wife agreed; "in the meantime I'll mend some clothes." And she sat down at the sewing-machine.

Uncle Krystof lived in an old house in the Nove Mesto section of Prague. It was a gray building, quiet and paunchy. Its arcade vaulted over a narrow sidewalk; for years, a blind man with a pale, motionless face had been sitting under one of the arches with his legs crossed like those of a fakir and his outstretched arm holding a matchbox.

The front of the house was decorated by two wooder horses' heads. The heads laughed derisively, revealir huge teeth. On the ground floor was a company dealin harness equipment. The firm bore an old-fashioned Florian Lenz.

The house yawned with its arched entrancew which moldy coolness wafted, even in summer contained several crates, an overturned han sickly fig tree in a wooden flowerpot. The so surrounded by glass-enclosed back porcl clinging runners of ivy and the bluish flor Old inhabitants whose era had pass behind those glass porches; their v he hissed. "All right, then. But remember, I'll get even with you. You'll regret this, you useless scarecrow."

The oven man hugged the pants to his chest and shouted, trembling before the furious policeman like a rabbit before a snake: "I won't sell, I won't. . ."

"I could confiscate that suit," the policeman shouted, "because you obtained it without my knowledge from one of my tenants . . . Tenants are not allowed to hand out gifts without the landlord's permission. That's the way the ordinance reads . . . It's very nice of you to gang up with the tenants against your own brother-in-law. All right, all right . . . But don't you dare set foot in my house. If I see you, I'll unleash the dog on you, you louse. . .!"

And the policeman slammed the door behind him.

Trotting back home, he wheezed, red-faced as a copper skillet: "I won't permit it, I f-forbid it, I w-won't stand for it. . ."

rustling of paper, and their steps were muffled by felt slippers.

2   The old house belonged to Uncle Krystof. Every three months, the white-haired tenants gathered at his place, bringing their rent and receiving from the landlord a glass of chocolate liqueur. After they had inquired as to each other's health, they went back to their apartments. Uncle Krystof kept the money in his medicine cabinet. From time to time he used some of it to buy savings certificates.

The clerk climbed the stone stairway to the second floor and stopped in front of a door bearing an enameled sign with the name Christoph Otto Kunstmuller embossed in old-fashioned German script. He pulled on the wooden handle and heard the thin tinkle of a bell. For a long time nobody came to the door. Then there was the sound of footsteps and the clerk noticed that the peephole in the door was slowly opening. Behind such doors, fitted with tinkly doorbells, lived frightened people who learned from newspapers that the world was full of itinerant criminals ready to pounce on their property. A morose housekeeper gave the visitor a suspicious once-over and hesitatingly let him be admitted.

The old man was sitting in his armchair, embroidering some sort of quilt with multicolored silk. Leathery-faced gentlemen with tall black collars looked down from their narrow frames. A scraggly parrot in a gilded cage gave the clerk a sideways glance and suddenly shouted in a strong voice: "Ach-tung!"

Mr. Syrovy greeted his uncle, who put away his needlework, took off his glasses, and peered at his nephew. He didn't seem to recognize him. The clerk pronounced his name. With a jubilant cry the old man struggled to his feet and with trembling arms embraced the visitor. He called out: "Greetings, Ferdinand! How is your wife, Valerie?" The oldster invariably mistook his nephew for some other member of his many-branched family. This time he took him for his cousin Ferdinand, who had been a sergeant with the Pardubice dragoons and died at the turn of the century. It took the clerk a lot of effort to convince his uncle that he wasn't Ferdinand but the son of Joseph, a nephew on his mother's side. Uncle's mind was fogged by age, and past events were mixed up in bizarre confusion. He barely understood the genealogic explanation and kept sighing: "How the time passes! Just imagine!" And the parrot again screamed: "Ach-tung!"

Then Uncle winked conspiratorially, dragged himself with difficulty to his safety box, opened it, and from a small iron box took out a handful of mint candies, which he pressed into his nephew's hand.

"Eat," he said; "those are medicinal pastilles. They'll refresh you, and your mind will stay clear the whole day. I am giving them to you because you're my favorite. If I like someone, I show it. . ."

The old man became cheerful. The clerk shifted the tasteless candy around his mouth and tried to follow the old man's narrative, which droned on with the monotonous burble of rain running down a drainpipe. Uncle was recounting the attack on Sarajevo. Then his recollections suddenly shifted to some mountains: He and his wife are riding in a sleigh through a snowy countryside. His wife has birthpangs and is moaning. And a pack of hungry wolves is racing after them. The eyes of the furious beasts phosphoresce in the darkness of the night. A single moment of delay means certain disaster. In the course of the story, however, the clerk learned that this terrible event did not involve his uncle at all, but a certain stationmaster who died of typhoid fever in Srem.

"That occurred in the seventies," Uncle added. "Pick up that thick book, it's all described there. That year there was an extremely cruel winter and all the birds froze to death. You'll find that in the book, too, for everything that ever happened is there. I don't want you to think that I am exaggerating. . ."

"Yes. . ." Uncle sighed after a while. "A lot of strange things have happened . . . But I wish I knew what happened to that book. They steal everything on you if you're not careful . . . And I wanted to know the height of the Vendome column . . . There was a picture of it in the book. And now there is no way of getting information . . . You wouldn't by any chance know, Otto, the height of the Vendome column?"

The clerk didn't know.

"Too bad," said the old man. He became lost in thought, then said: "Ask one of your friends and then tell me . . . Do that. . ."

Suddenly he gave a lively start. "Good Lord," he exclaimed, "I almost forgot. Have you seen this?"

He showed the clerk a small box with a piece of some black mineral.

"You know what that is? You don't? That's petrified wheat from Tetin. A great rarity. Scholars wanted to give me a pile of money for it. But I won't give it up, I know its value. . ."

The old man chattered on and on. The clerk found himself a captive of cruel boredom. He tried to think of a way out. At last he got up and announced that he had to go.

Uncle turned nervous.

"Catherine," he called toward the kitchen, "give Gabriel a piece of pastry for the road. Wrap up a piece for him, in

case he gets hungry on the road. That's right . . . Yes . . .
And come to see me again, I am very lonely. . ."

3   The clerk heaved a deep sigh when he found
himself out in the street. He felt as if he had just left the
nineteenth century and re-entered our era. He walked to
the streetcar stop and waited for his tram. The evening
brought no relief after the sweltering Prague summer day.
Streams of people returning from outings, covered with the
dust of roads, poured out of the railroad station. Men with
knapsacks on their backs, swinging walking sticks; women
with tanned necks and bunches of wildflowers in their
arms. Motorcycles driven by bank employees droned
through the streets; pressed up behind them were girls in
tight pants, wearing flat caps. The couples looked like
paired butterflies in flight.

The trams were jammed with people holding on to
leather straps and swaying from side to side. Conductors
elbowed their way among them, clicking their ticket-
punchers. The cars resounded with loud conversation and
the crying of sleepy children. The seats were taken by
portly women with preoccupied looks and their husbands
with white vests and close-shaven faces. Out on the
platforms stood lovers, submerged into each other,
convinced that they had not yet told each other everything
they had been planning to say during the day. A man
carrying an ironing board got on and fumbled through his
pockets for small change. The tram crossed the bridge,
making a dark booming sound. The black water of the
river rippled gently. The clerk succeeded in getting a seat.
He sat wearily down and gazed at the reflection of fellow
passengers in the tram window. The man with the ironing
board, unnaturally tall, seemed to be quietly gliding past
the fronts of the shops.

On the other side of the bridge the tram filled up with mustachioed men, women carrying waxcloth shopping bags, and adolescents with cigarette stubs behind their ears. The conductors began to lose their official demeanor. They handed out tickets as they joked with the passengers and chatted with them about their domestic affairs. The tram passed the yellowed walls of factory buildings. From the gas works with its enormous tank emanated the sweetish smell of gas. The widespread domain of the railroad station came into view down below. Locomotives belched fiery columns of sparks, the thump of colliding bumpers rang out. The bitter aroma of black elder wafted from the poorhouse garden.

The clerk got off at the last stop. A group of youths stood under a streetlamp, their heads close together; the hunchback was in their midst. The clerk speeded up his steps. "I'll inform the policeman," he decided; " they're always up to something. Let him chase them away from our neighborhood. . ."

4   The house was dark; when he turned on the light, he saw that his wife was lying on the couch with a towel wrapped around her forehead.

"Are you sick?" asked the clerk.

"I have a bit of a headache," his wife said in a weak voice. "Your supper is in the oven . . . heat it up. . ."

The clerk took off his coat, hung it on the hanger and carefully put it away in the closet. He heard sobbing from the other room.

"What happened?" the clerk asked, worried. "Why are you crying?"

His wife didn't answer. She sobbed, and tears ran down her cheeks.

"He . . . the policeman . . . people gathered, and still he

raged . . . he said he'd been silent for a long time, but we have taken advantage of his kindness . . . and now he'll show us what he can do. . ."

"Who? Who was in a rage?" Syrovy wanted to know.

"Him . . . the policeman . . . people gathered, but he yelled all the more when he saw them listening . . . He said we are too uppity, nobody is good enough for us, but actually we're just official riff-raff. . ."

"But why? What made him carry on like that?"

"He said that I. . . that I demanded that the landlady help me close the window . . . 'Wench,' he screamed at me, 'how dare you ask such a thing? Don't you realize a land-lady is entitled to respect. . .?' Then he reproached me for having helped us to put the dresser in place, when we moved in; 'I am nobody's servant,' he said. He said he had thought we were loyal to him and didn't expect us to gang up against him with his brother-in-law. . ."

The clerk was horrified. "Is that right? He dared call you 'wench'? Well, calm down, stop crying . . . I'll have a talk with him. I'll give him a piece of my mind. 'Mister,' I'll say to him, 'I heard from my wife that you used some rough language on her. Mister! Don't you know the proper way to talk to a lady? I regret to say that I'm disappointed in you. . .'"

He pulled himself up and continued, waving his arms: " 'You apparently don't know, mister, whom you're deal-ing with. I'll take the necessary steps to teach you some manners. . .' Don't worry, Marie, I'll let him have it. . ."

"Ill fix him, I'll fix him," he mumbled, lying down on the bed.

Chapter Twenty-one

1   For some time, the policeman had been feeling a dark pressure in his insides, as if he had swallowed a large coat-button. He formulated his state to himself thus: "I'm so mad at the Syrovys I could burst."

One day it occurred to him that the Syrovys were occupying his house without paying rent. Somehow he seemed to have forgotten that the clerk had turned over to him his wife's dowry in return for rent-free use of the house for four years. But when the quarter was up, he realized bitterly that the other two tenant families were contributing toward the growth of his property, whereas the clerk wasn't.

"They sit in my house," he reflected angrily, "and it profits me nothing. Lousy freeloaders!"

"If they decided to move out," he speculated, "it would be to my advantage . . . I could get twenty-five thousand for their apartment . . . What am I saying, I could even get thirty . . . That would add up to quite a down payment. And on top of that, the new tenant would pay rent, even though it would be a bit lower. This way I get nothing. I am being cheated, badly cheated, damn it. . ."

And he clenched his fists and muttered angry words. The policeman had become a victim of that peculiar mental state to which landlords are subject. When a landlord signs a lease with a tenant, at first he sees it as a simple business proposition. But as soon as the tenant moves in with his belongings, the landlord begins to feel the tenant's presence as an imposition and an encroachment upon his private property.

There are many reasons why landlords feel enmity toward their tenants. Tenants are as a rule noisy. If they aren't noisy, they are suspect: surely they are silently thinking of ways to do damage to the landlord. They tend to have children and small animals. The landlord must hire a super. And these circumstances hinder good relations between the two parties. Then, too, tenants do not show the required measure of respect toward their landlords.

2   In the afternoon, the policeman was again working on his house. He was using concrete bricks to make a wall along the stairs, resembling the crenelated battlement of a medieval castle. He was thinking what sort of fence was needed to separate his property from the rest of the world. He decided on a barbed-wire barrier, which is the safest defense against the intrusions of trouble-makers.

The clerk stepped out on the terrace and saw the landlord squatting down to pick up a trowelful of mortar. He felt his chest tighten. But he tried to gather courage, recalling how roughly the policeman had treated his wife.

"It is necessary to tell him my opinion. I won't use vulgar words, nor will I let myself be provoked into shouting. Simple folk often go astray and don't know how to keep themselves in check. I will remind him that we are educated people and that education must be respected. But I'll speak clearly, distinctly, and energetically."

He stepped up to the policeman and greeted him.

The policeman murmured something and wiped his brow with his sleeve without glancing at the tenant. He tapped the last brick to make sure it was firmly in place and then vigorously smoothed down the mortar.

The clerk shifted his feet uneasily and then remarked on the progress of the policeman's handiwork.

The policeman suddenly threw down the trowel and stood up. He looked the clerk sharply in the eye and said: "This is what I wanted to tell you, Mr. Syrovy. I am fed up. It makes me mad when I see that my orders are ignored. I am a mild person, but I won't stand for pigheadedness. As they say, enough is enough. . ."

The clerk started to say something, but the policeman interrupted him.

"A landlord is nobody's slave," he continued, "and anybody who wants to fool around with me is not going to get very far. I've kept silent for too long, thinking: maybe they'll learn. But if there is no change for the better, look out!"

"I don't understand," the official countered; "what have we done? What has incited your anger?"

"What's that?" the landlord exploded. "You have the nerve to ask? You think it's all right for your woman to dump garbage in the yard? Am I supposed to clean it up? Am I your servant? Garbage belongs in a can, which is to be turned over to the garbage man. That's how things are done. . ."

"Excuse me," said the offended clerk, "don't refer to my wife as 'your woman'. . ."

"Well then, your wife," said the policeman with irony, "or your lady, for God's sake! I don't take that honor away from her. But if she wants to be a lady in my eyes, then she has to obey the house rules. That's how it is, mister."

He cleared his throat and spat.

"As far as you are concerned, Mr. Syrovy," he said in a milder tone, "I have nothing against you. Not at all. It would be a sin to hurt you, you are such a quiet person. I'd be prepared to get up at midnight to have a chat with you. You have my full respect. But you don't know what's going on, you're away all day at the office. Oh, if you only knew what goes on here! There are times when I feel like dropping everything and walking out. . ."

He squatted down once again and continued his work.

The clerk was nonplused and didn't know what to add. Then he offered the landlord a cigarette. The policeman muttered his thanks, put the cigarette behind his ear, and devoted himself to his work, ignoring the clerk's presence.

The tenant left, pondering the outcome of his mission. He felt rather dissatisfied with himself.

"I should have expressed my opinion in a stronger manner," he thought to himself. "It was up to me to say: 'Mister landlord, I urge you to show more restraint in your expressions and your tone. If you admit your error, then we can remain good friends. . .' But he is satisfied with me. I get along with everybody."

3   The policeman stood up and went into the garden. Restlessness drove him away from his work. He was bursting with anger.

"Why did I listen to that numskull?" he wheezed. "Why didn't I let him have it? Why am I such a softie? They drink my blood and I let them, like a ninny. And then go and accept a cigarette from him. Shame on me!"

He paced the paths around the flower beds. The gravel crunched under his feet. He stopped in front of a pink bush, noticing that the bast strip that tied the trunk to the pole had come loose. The bush had produced a single rose, yellow and gorgeous. He bent down and smelled the flower with half-closed eyes.

"A beautiful rose blooms in my garden," he rejoiced, "but the tailor's roses are shabby. I'll bet this year not a single one of them is going to bloom." Then he suddenly remembered that the Syrovys would be living in his house for the next four years.

He moaned: "What good is a rose, when I'm such a nincompoop! Mecl the tailor got a down payment of thirty-five thousand for his hole in the wall, and he still collects rent. Just take a look at him! Such a nobody, and yet he's got a head on him like a silver bell. He knows how to turn everything to his profit. Such a one doesn't need roses; all he cares about is the silver ringing in his pockets."

He stopped to calm his seething blood. Then he came to a decision and waved his right arm in a sweeping gesture.

"The tenants' flower beds will be abolished. The whole garden will be mine. The tailor didn't give his tenants a piece of his garden either, because he is careful. You're not going to cut me to pieces. You're not going to grow fat on my flesh and blood. No more mister soft-heart, no sir . . . The garden is mine, and if anybody doesn't like it let him go to the devil. That's where I stand. . ."

He examined the young apple tree and saw that the apple was thriving, filling out.

"More power to you, my apple," he addressed the fruit tenderly. "You're mine; nobody else is allowed to eat you . . . The garden, too, is mine, and the house is mine. And everything existing here is subject to my will. . ."

4   The clerk told his wife: "I spoke to him. And I gave him a piece of my mind."

"What did he have to say?" his wife asked.

"What could he say? He saw that he was in the wrong. I believe the whole thing was just a misunderstanding."

"Misunderstanding. . ." his wife answered morosely, "what kind of misunderstanding, when he yelled at me as if I was some sort of. . . Did you tell him not to call me 'wench'?"

"Everything will be all right," the clerk said evasively; "but he did remark that you shouldn't dump garbage in the yard. He said that the garbage belongs on the garbage-man's cart. He is upset by any kind of disorder. . ."

"How do you like that!" his wife exclaimed. "He himself told me, when we first moved in: 'Madam, don't bother carrying the garbage across the street. By all means dump it in the yard. I'll take care of it. . .' At that time it was hard to cross the street because of the piles of mud . . . And now he shoots off his mouth at us. . ."

"Everything will be all right," the clerk repeated soothingly; "there's always problems. We have to compromise with one another. The main thing is to have peace in the house."

"You know me," his wife said: "I'm not the kind of person to look for quarrels. But I won't stand for anyone shouting at me."

She went to the bathroom and returned with a wicker basket.

"I'm going to fetch the laundry," she said; "stay home in the meantime and mind the house."

She walked out the door. The clerk stepped over to the window and pensively drummed a march on the pane.

Chapter Twenty-two

1   It was a dark night, calm and sultry as is common toward the end of July. The horn of the moon was swallowed up by shreds of clouds hanging over the horizon. Everything was asleep except for the cats restlessly wandering over the roofs, emitting penetrating shrieks. Dogs answered with languid, prolonged howling. From the Corner Tavern came drunken voices and the clang of a player piano; it was the night before payday. Now and again a late-hour reveler dragged himself home on wobbly legs along the row of houses, gesticulating with his arms and muttering muddled words to himself.

Yet in the policeman's garden a man was busy at work. He dug, swung his shovel, energetically stamped down the soil. He finished his work, went down to the cellar, and locked up his tools. Then he put on his cap and jacket, said: "That's that!" and left.

In the morning Mrs. Syrovy went to the garden to get fresh vegetables for her kitchen. She was astounded to find her beds completely ruined. Uprooted vegetables lay on the paths. Pansies, carnations, and herbs were dying, stamped into the ground. Only the currant and gooseberry bushes remained unharmed. Mrs. Syrovy's shocked exclamation fetched her husband. They stood helplessly over this desolation.

"Well, there it is," Mrs. Syrovy said, utterly dejected.

"Who could have done such a thing?" the clerk wondered glumly.

"Who. . .?" his wife said in a choking voice. "Who else but that. . ."

"Hush," the clerk hissed, "don't you dare! You haven't seen anyone. Keep quiet or there'll be a disaster!"

"I know what I'm talking about," the wife defended herself; "nobody else could have done it. . ."

"I beg you on my knees, be quiet! We don't have the right to accuse anyone . . . Better to suffer wrongs than bring on more trouble. . ."

"What malice!" he moaned, and he went back into the house.

2 On being informed of the incident, the policeman snorted and came to the garden. At the site of the deed he found the gathered tenants, who were expressing their opinions about the mischief.

Frowning, the policeman circled the devastated beds.

He said: "Call me Max if I didn't expect something like this to happen."

"We didn't expect anything like this," said Mrs. Syrovy.

"And yet you were just the people who should have expected it," said the policeman derisively.

"What do you mean by that?" asked Mrs. Syrovy.

"I mean. . . what I mean," answered the policeman, winking slyly at the gathered tenants.

"That's what you get for giving some people a garden," he added. "That's the thanks you get for everything."

"What are you hinting at?" Mrs. Syrovy raised her voice.

"I'm not hinting. I know everything."

"What do you know?" Mrs. Syrovy insisted.

"Never mind, woman."

"Why don't you say it straight out, that we ourselves caused the damage."

"Never mind, woman."

144

"I resent your insinuations. This is unheard of!" exclaimed Mrs. Syrovy.

"I'm fed up with the entire business," said the policeman. "I am going to take steps now. I won't let my property be destroyed. The garden will be closed and no one will be allowed access. That's my decision."

"We'll see about that," shouted Mrs. Syrovy. "According to the contract, we have the use of the garden."

"You can stick your contract. . ." and the policeman made an indecent gesture. "The garden is mine, understand? I am master here. I rule over everything. Nobody is my superior. What I decide will stand. The garden will be closed and that's that."

"That isn't fair! We haven't done anything," other tenants objected bashfully.

"You see, my friends. . ." said the policeman. "All for one and one for all. That's how the world runs. When the tenants don't get along with each other, then the landlord has to intervene."

"Who doesn't get along?" Mrs. Syrovy countered angrily.

"Never mind, woman."

3   The policeman worked all afternoon. Toward evening the entrance to the garden was closed by a gate with iron bars. In front of the gate he set up a wooden pole with a sign visible from afar:

ENTRANCE BY UNAUTHORIZED PERSONS STRICTLY PROHIBITED

And underneath:

According to the directive of the owner, beginning this day, the garden will be locked. The key will be in the landlord's possession at all times, and tenants intending to work on their plots will announce their intention to the owner, who will lend them the key. The key will be available daily between the hours of eight and nine in the morning. The tenants are obliged to return the key in due time and to inform the landlord of their activity.

JAN FAKTOR, owner.

After finishing his work, the policeman stepped back a few feet and silently read the sign to himself. His eyes burned with a fire kindled by the sense of private ownership. He said to himself: "I composed that well. I'm no slouch. I know how things are done. Now I'll throw the book at them, to teach them that kindness has its limits."

He saw a couple of sparrows hopping around the vegetable beds. He cursed, picked up a stick, and flung it at the birds. He was seized by anger because the birds were transgressing the boundaries of his land without permission; and because his rule did not extend to birds.

"What nerve!" he rasped angrily.

He decided to get himself a shotgun and start exterminating the sparrows.

"Whoever willfully touches my property will pay with his head."

4   The news dealer's wife entered the yard in order to split some wood.

The policeman pointed at the sign with the warning inscription and asked: "How does it appeal to you?"

"I like it," the tenant whispered.

The policeman looked her suspiciously in the eye.

"You say it as if you didn't really mean it. Watch yourself."

"I do like it, for heaven's sake!" she exclaimed anxiously.

"That's better!" the policeman said with satisfaction. "If

anybody doesn't like my regulations, I'll give them a hard time."

And after a short pause: "I've wanted to talk to you for a long time . . . I have the greatest confidence in you, even though you pay the lowest rent. I can't keep watch over every nook and cranny, that's obvious. That's why I am asking you to report every odd event that happens in the house. Especially if someone expresses improper opinions about me. Are you willing?"

"As you wish," replied the tenant.

"Good. It will be to your benefit. I'll show my favor. Do it to me, and I'll do it to you. Hmmm . . . That Mrs. Syrovy . . . has she ever said anything bad about me?"

"Not that I've heard," answered the news dealer's wife.

"She's never called me a ruffian, a vulgarian, or anything of that sort?"

"Not that I know of."

"Or a big-mouth, a usurer, a scoundrel?"

"I couldn't say."

"Hmm . . . You don't seem very sincere. On the other hand, I can tell you that she never says a kind word about you. When you were first moving in, she declared that you must be some sort of impoverished riffraff. She turned up her nose at your furniture: 'It's made of soft wood. I hope they didn't bring bed-bugs into the house.' "

"Jesus!" moaned the tenant. "How could she say such a thing! Our place is so clean the president himself wouldn't be ashamed to spend the night with us. What a gossip! That's the limit!"

"Yes, that's the limit . . . And all the time she pretends to be so friendly. . ."

"Those are the people you've got to watch," the policeman instructed.

After she left, the policeman choked with quiet laughter.

"There is a law," he said to himself, "that tenants who habitually fail to get along with fellow tenants can be duly evicted."

Chapter Twenty-three

1   The policeman's mother died. She'd been a familiar figure in the neighborhood, always walking doubled over like an old willow. She was in the habit of trailing carts loaded with coal, the way dolphins trail the wake of a ship. She gleaned bits of coal that fell off the back of the cart and gathered them in a basket, weighing down her rounded back. Her eyes, fixed on the pavement, searched the ground like sparrows inspecting piles of horse droppings.

The corner of a sort of shed had been reserved for her. There she spent her nights on a bed covered by rags and a torn horse blanket. She did odd jobs around the neighborhood and washed the laundry for her son's family, for the policeman demanded that she be useful to the day she died. In return, he provided shelter. She was fed by neighbors. Whatever money she earned, the policeman took away from her, maintaining that she would only lose it.

Her husband lived in a cottage in the village. He rarely saw his wife, for the policeman resented visits. He didn't want anyone prying into his affairs. Relatives bring nothing but malicious talk and trouble, he would say.

His mother's death saddened the policeman. When he compared the cost of maintaining the old woman against the profit he derived from her work, he realized that he had suffered a loss.

"There is no help for it," he sighed; "she's gone. Nothing can be done about it." But then he remembered the news dealer's wife and his face brightened: "Sure! Why didn't I think of it before? That woman will do our laundry. She won't dare oppose my wishes."

He frowned when he thought of the expenses connected with the funeral, for he intended to provide a showy event, as befitted a house-owner. His reputation mustn't suffer on account of miserly funeral arrangements. But he rejected the offer of the funeral parlor, which promised to provide him fair and reliable service. Being in essence an enterprising spirit, he decided to handle the funeral himself. He negotiated with the cabinet-maker for a casket, and gained a reduction in price. Musicians threw up their hands and swore and pleaded, but in the end they lowered their fee. The priest, too, proved obliging, after the policeman slyly pleaded poverty. He was glad to see that in this way the funeral would cost fifty per cent less than the figure cited by the funeral parlor.

"Let's face it," he thought to himself with deep satisfaction, "you won't find many as smart as me. Nobody gets the better of me."

He had to do a lot of searching and running. It turned out that the government does not easily release its citizens to the other world; it keeps careful records on everyone.

"How lucky," thought the policeman, "that I am more or less finished with the house. Otherwise I couldn't afford to waste so much time on this nonsense."

He pondered whether to ask his father and brother-in-law to contribute to the funeral expenses. But then he waved the idea off. Those beggars! Pennypinchers! He could just imagine their moaning and groaning. So be it. But some occasion for recouping his expenses was sure to arise.

"Do it to me, and I'll do it to you," that's what he always said.

2   The day of the funeral arrived. Women gathered in front of the house, their hands under their aprons. They talked about the characteristics of the deceased and about the fact that we all must go one day. The policeman's father came and filled the room with lament. The eyes of the laconic brother-in-law teared up as usual. The policeman's wife keened with limitless sorrow. At the same time, however, her sharp eyes kept watch over the children to make sure they didn't cause any mischief that might disturb the dignified character of the proceedings.

The policeman scurries to and fro, maintaining order and keeping track of the people who have come to the ceremony. The participants in the funeral gather. Here comes the grocer Mejstrik, he shakes the policeman's hand and stutters words of condolence. He is neatly dressed and wears a grave expression. The house fills up with friends and acquaintances; they all display the policeman's popularity. At last the tenants appear. The news dealer's wife wrapped in a black shawl, the teacher Soltys with his spouse. The policeman notices the absence of the Syrovys. He frowns vengefully: "I won't forget this!"

The hearse rattles to a stop in front of the house. The lean horses chew on their bits and shake their black plumes. The musicians arrive, wearing blue vizored caps. The brass of their instruments sparkles with a meticulous shine. The priest arrives, a square biretta on his bald head and bags under his eyes. Cemetery employees carry the coffin. Their mourning livery hangs loose, drooping and cynical.

The procession is forming, with the musicians in the vanguard. The acolyte, carrying a cross, walks ahead of the procession. When the wind parts his gown, his naked knees and boy-scout pants are clearly visible. "Boom. . . boom . . . boomboom . . . tralala. . ." the music rings out. The procession snakes through the streets. It turns up a road lined by dilapidated buildings. On top of the hill is the cemetery where the dead of this quarter are put to rest.

The policeman walks behind the coffin, his nose submerged in a handkerchief. He is thinking about the electric bell that would have to be installed in the house. "More expenses, damn it," he sighs. "And how come the musicians aren't playing? They're supposed to play, their snouts can't be that tired, they sure took enough money . . . From our house all the way to the cemetery they played a total of three pieces and they think they're done. Three pieces, that's all . . . Thieves, scoundrels, miserable cheats! I'll have to knock down their fee, so they don't think they're dealing with a ninny. . ."

The rites begin. The priest sprinkles the coffin and recites Latin words. "*Lux aeterna luceat ei,*" he intones in an oily, ecclesiastic baritone. In an undertone, the mourners repeat after him the Our Father.

"Sure, why not," the policeman grumbles enviously, "he mutters a few words and expects fifty crowns for it. Some business!" He leans over the grave to throw a clod of earth on the coffin. At the same time he measures the depth of the pit. "Two men worked on this for three days," he mutters malignantly; "I'd get it done in one afternoon. Oh Lord . . . I am helpless before the world's thievery."

3   The funeral participants parted and the police-man retired with his father and his brother-in-law to the Corner Tavern. They sat down at a table covered with a red checkerboard tablecloth. The policeman ordered three beers, for today he was determined to show off his generosity.

Father gazed into his glass, wiped the foam off his beard with his palm, and sighed: "Poor Mother . . . Now she's gone. . ."

"Too bad," the brother-in-law chimed in.

"There's no help for it," remarked the son; "we can't change it." He ordered another beer, for his throat was dry. And then a third and a fourth. He became pretty tipsy, and began to hold forth.

"I wonder if you know," he said, "that I could have you arrested at one fell swoop. The two of you, as you sit here."

"How come," Father said, startled; "we haven't done anything wrong."

"That so?" said the in-law.

"Don't worry, I won't arrest you," the policeman calmed them down. "I was only giving you a for-instance."

"Not a chance," the old man smiled. "If someone behaves himself he can't be arrested."

"That's how much you know, Dad," the policeman replied with contempt. "You don't understand a thing. You don't know a policeman's power. A policeman, my dear fellows, only has to say the word and that's that."

The old man shook his head doubtfully: "For instance, you come up to me and say: 'You come along with me, because you killed this here Alois.' But it isn't true, because I didn't kill anybody. Are you trying to tell me you could arrest me anyway and they'd hang me just on your say-so?"

"You bet, if it came to that." The policeman shouted and

pounded the table with his fist. "I just snap handcuffs on you and off we go to the station. There I line you up in front of the desk and salute: 'Commissioner, sir, beg to report that I caught this person in the act of robbery and murder.' 'I see,' the commissioner answers, 'another one of those. To the slammer with the rascal!' And before you can say 'Holy Wenceslas' you're sitting in the cooler. As simple as that."

The policeman lifted his glass and took a deep swig.

"Listen," he continued after putting the glass back down on the table, "I know all sorts of strange cases. We have our way of handling these things. 'Did you do it?' — 'No, sir.' Bang, right on his snout. We ask a second time. 'No, sir.' 'No?' Bang, right on his snout. And so on. The interrogation continues. — 'Yes, sir.' That's better. Why couldn't you have said that before? You would have saved us a lot of work. — Sure, that's how it goes. What would you know. . ."

"Go on," muttered Father, "the suds have gone to your head. You don't know what you're talking about. It makes me laugh, listening to you. I know you're a big shot, but you're not such a big shot to be able to do anything you please. There are even bigger shots on top of you. Not even policemen can do anything they please. Stop pontificating and let's go home. We don't want to embarrass ourselves in public."

"Sure, sure, don't you worry," babbled the policeman, "but first I'll have one more for the road. I can afford it. I've got more than all of you put together. I am a landlord and you are beggars. You never gave me anything. You chased me out into the cold when I was just a child: find your own livelihood. I built myself a most beautiful house. I pulled myself up to the top. I'll throw out the tenants and get myself new ones who'll be more appreciative. It's not balconies that count, but harmony in the house. That bastard of a tailor will curse the day when he got it in his noggin to build balconies. Anybody who crosses me will pay for it. I can be a real swine, take my word for it. . ."

He pounded the table: "And Syrovy's got to go, right away, this minute! I am not going to watch him lording it over me and not paying any rent. I'll make him scoot double-time. . ."

"That measly dwarf," brother-in-law chimed in angrily; he couldn't forgive the clerk his small stature, as a result of which the gift suit didn't fit.

"And when I told you he was a dwarf, you argued with me," retorted the policeman. "You think I wanted that suit? I just want harmony in the family; let nobody say we don't stick together . . . So what's the story, will I get the suit?"

"Oh, no," answered the laconic man.

"But you can't even wear it. Or do you think it's going to grow a couple of sizes?"

"Never mind," the laconic man insisted, "it's about time I had something nice, too. . ."

"All right then. But I see through you. You have it all wrong. You try to ape me, because you want to measure up to me. When I got me a goat, right away you had to have two goats, just so you could trump me. And both of them croaked, and now you and your goats can go chase each other. You're all a fine bunch. . ."

He was flushed and his eyes turned bloodshot. The old man gave the in-law a nudge, and both of them quietly slipped out of the tavern.

4 By the time the policeman reached his house, the thought of the expenses incurred in the tavern had sobered him up. When he saw a group of women and children seated in front of his gate, he called out in a loud voice: "Go home, folks. There's nothing going on here. All of you should mind your own business."

The women got up and left, protesting under their breath. The policeman then climbed to the room under the attic. He found the news dealer's wife standing in front of the stove. He said: "I have resolved as follows: My poor mother has, unfortunately, died. And I have decided to put up a splendid monument to her, even if it costs a fortune. I'll plant the grave with beautiful flowers. And you will visit the grave every day, fill the lamp with oil, and water the flowers."

The news dealer's wife agreed.

"And from now on, you will do the laundry for us, in memory of the poor deceased."

The tenant did not object.

"Yes, yes. . ." the landlord melancholically shook his head. "Where are you, Mother of mine? She was a good woman. I suffered a loss on account of her leaving us. I have to find ways to repair this loss. . ."

He reached for the door-handle.

"And you'll report every little whisper that you hear in the house," he added. "Brief and to the point. I appoint you the house overseer."

Chapter Twenty-four

1   "I want this mess out of here right now!" the landlord shouted into the hallway.

"You hear me? Are you deaf?" he repeated when there wasn't any answer.

Only then did Mrs. Syrovy understand that the shouts were addressed to her. Anxiously, she stepped out on the terrace.

She found the policeman standing there, arms akimbo, his red face full of anger.

"What's this?" he pointed to the ground.

The rust-colored cat lay on the terrace floor with bared canines and glassy eyes.

"How long is this carcass going to lie here?" yelled the policeman. "Am I, the landlord, supposed to clean up after you?"

"Poor Micinka," Mrs. Syrovy whispered, bending over the dead cat. "So your turn has come, already. . ."

"How about it?" the landlord clamored. "Are you going to leave it here for decoration?"

Amina, seeing that her enemy was dead, went into a merry dance in front of the dog-house, rearing up and pulling at her chain.

"Even the poor animal was in someone's way. . ." Mrs. Syrovy said.

"What is that supposed to mean?" the policeman challenged.

"Nothing. . ."

"That's better. Watch your tongue. I understand your insinuations."

"After all. . ."

"Be careful! I know what you're thinking."

"What I am thinking is my business, not yours."

"You. . . Don't push me too far . . . Don't shoot your trap off at a landlord . . . And anyhow . . . That beast had it coming. She caused all sorts of mischief and injured my dog. I won't let my property be ruined."

"Micinka was just like us. When she was left in peace, she didn't bother a soul. . ."

"I know," the policeman derided her, "you're quite a pair, you and your cat. . ."

Mrs. Syrovy didn't respond.

The policeman stared at her, then waved his arm and left, muttering angrily.

Mrs. Syrovy fetched a spade, dug a hole, and buried the cat. Tears ran down her face.

"Yes, poor Micinka," she sobbed, "a house where they kill animals is no place for people, either. . ."

As she passed the dog-house, Amina bared her teeth and growled: "Tenants are not going to lord it over us. Here we are the masters!"

"Sit!" the tenant shouted.

The animal took fright and sought refuge in the dog-house.

2   That afternoon, the policeman was getting ready to go on duty when he received a report that Mrs. Syrovy had a visitor. He dropped everything and trotted back to his house. He stopped in the hall and listened behind the door.

"How beautiful it is here," said Mrs. Syrovy's cousin. She added: "The garden is in full bloom. It smells as nice as an apothecary. And how quiet it is all around. Really, it's like paradise, my dear girl. What bliss for my nerves, my poor nerves. . ."

Mrs. Syrovy sighed. "You want it with milk or without?"

"With milk," answered the ruddy-faced woman. "And your milk is so tasty, so natural, real country milk. Some people are lucky, but I. . . I am very unhappy. When I go to bed at night, I pray the good Lord to rid me of my landlord. Such a tyrant, I can't even tell you. The other day he got it in his head that on Fridays, Saturdays, and Sundays nobody is allowed in the attic."

"But why?"

"Who knows. Just got it in his head. On Fridays, Saturdays, and Sundays he simply refuses to give the tenants the key to the attic. Just imagine. Our apartment is small, so we had to store some things in the attic. And now we can't get to them three days in the week. Just on account of his pigheadedness. My husband asked a lawyer what to do. Sue him, he said, for breaking the lease. That's easy to say. Where would we get the money for a lawsuit? So people just try to avoid trouble. . ."

"There's no law for landlords," Mrs. Syrovy said quietly.

"And so I often wish for the good Lord to take me away, because this life is really unbearable. . ."

The ensuing silence was shattered by violent noise. Somebody pounded on the door and screamed: "Out!"

Mrs. Syrovy staggered. Her cousin turned pale. "What's going on?" she asked in a trembling voice.

Before Mrs. Syrovy could answer, the policeman burst into the room.

"Well?" he thundered imperiously. "How long do I have to wait? I'm telling you: this woman's got to leave!"

"Excuse me. . ." the ruddy-faced lady protested.

The policeman pointed at the door. "No 'excuse me,' just

pick up your things and get out! I don't tolerate visitors in the house. So how about it?"

"Well, I never. . ."

"Don't talk so much, and get going. Go home to your mirrors and carpets. You don't like my house because it isn't luxurious enough for you. I don't let anybody slander my house. Get going!"

"What mirrors. . .? I just don't understand . . . how dare you insult me like that . . . Darling, tell me what makes him rage like that. . .?"

"Silence!" the policeman hissed, frothing at the mouth. "Out, out. . .!"

The cousin rose to her feet. "Never mind, I'm going . . . I feel sorry for you, Marinka. I see that you're even worse off than I . . . Shame on you, mister, shame, shame. . ."

"Not another word! Or I'll put you under arrest!"

Out on the street, when she saw the inscription:

> OH, HEART OF MAN,
> BECOME NOT THE HEART OF A PREDATOR!

she called out once more: "Shame, shame. . .!"

The policeman threw a clod of earth after her.

3   The same day, the policeman put up the following:

> TAKE NOTICE
> All tenants are hereby advised that outside persons are strictly prohibited from entering the house. Such visits will be permitted only in exceptional cases, and will require written notice by the tenant to the owner of the house 24 hours in advance. This written request will include: 1. Type of visit. 2. Purpose of visit. 3. How long the visitor intends to stay. Transgressions of this notice will be punished.
> JAN FAKTOR, owner

He made three copies of the notice and pasted them in the hall. That upset Mr. Soltys, the teacher, who interpreted this regulation as a step directed against him.

"How am I to understand this?" he asked the policeman. "I thought we had made an agreement that my brethren may visit me. . ."

"This does not apply to you, professor," the landlord soothed him. "You— you belong in a different class. You gather in order to perform spiritual exercises. And it is well known that spirits don't soil the stairs nor damage property in other ways. I have nothing against spirits. They don't gossip, they don't spread false rumors around the house, and they don't instigate against the landlord. People from the other world don't violate my rules. I therefore have no reason to intervene against them."

"I see, I see," said the teacher, relieved.

"You are good as gold and I know it. But as to the Syrovys, I'll chase them out of the house because they don't respect me. They don't treat me like a landlord."

"That's wrong, that is, of course, wrong." The teacher nodded his head.

"Well, everything in due course."

The policeman left and, walking down the street, said to himself: "Now for a three-ring circus like you've never seen before!"

4   With his head bowed, the clerk listened to his wife's report of the morning's events.

"Just think," she lamented, "the shame! Who would have thought . . . People were crowding around, I felt like hiding my head . . . So much money, all our savings, and we're living like inmates in a prison. And you can't get any justice. What a world. . ."

"He won't even let us have visitors. Soon he'll forbid us

to breathe. And the things he promised us! 'You'll live here like it was paradise . . . I'll permit you everything. . .' And now we're living in cruel slavery."

The clerk carefully opened the door and looked into the hall. Then he said: "I never trusted him. He seemed too friendly. His excessive friendliness conceals a base, calculating spirit. When you first put your hand in water, you can't tell for a second whether it's icy or scalding. We made a mistake. We fell into his trap. And now we're at his mercy. There is no hope for liberation; we don't have enough money. There is no freedom for poor people. . ."

"I'm worse off than you," moaned the wife. "You can at least escape to the office. But I have to bear his tyranny all day. Many times I've been afraid he'd strike me. I am here alone, without witnesses."

"I can't imagine he'd lose all self-control and hit a defenseless woman. And if he tried anything like that, take a look. . ." And he pointed out the window.

Under the streetlamp there was once again a gathering of youths, with the hunchback in their midst.

"You see them? They're outlaws. If the policeman ever attacks you, call them. They'll protect you. They're good boys, who are used to skirmishing with the police . . . And tomorrow I'll give him a good talking-to. You'll see. I'll tell him straight out . . . He'll get it this time, that villain's villain. . .!"

Chapter Twenty-five

1   In the morning Mrs. Syrovy wanted to go out, but the door wouldn't open, as if something was blocking it. She called her husband. The clerk jumped out of bed, and both of them leaned against the door. After a lengthy effort they finally succeeded in pushing it open and found a large, old-fashioned scale behind the door.

"How did that scale get there?" the wife wondered.

Perplexed, they examined the machine.

"What disorder!" the clerk complained. "Has anybody ever heard of such a thing? To put a scale right in front of the door? Somebody might easily have gotten hurt!"

Together, they pulled the scale out of the way.

"Mrs. Syrovy," a quiet voice was heard from upstairs, "that scale belongs to the landlord. I heard him saying to his wife: 'I'll put the scale in front of their door, just for fun.' I'm telling you so you know where you stand."

Then they heard the news dealer's wife carefully closing her door.

"Hardened criminal!" the clerk said angrily. "He spends the whole day thinking up ways of tormenting us. Scoundrel, rogue, good-for-nothing! He'll hear from me. The Lord knows he won't be laughing when he hears what I have to say. . ."

A dark shadow passed the window.

"Here he is," whispered Mrs. Syrovy.

"Good," the clerk said firmly. "I'm going out."

"For heaven's sake!" his wife gasped.

"Don't worry, I'll keep my head."

He went out.

The policeman was walking around, his face frowning and malignant. Angry thoughts filled his mind and convulsed his innards.

"Mr. Faktor," the clerk said in a quaking voice.

The policeman cupped his hand to his ear, as if he had trouble hearing.

"Mr. Faktor, in my opinion. . ." the clerk began again.

"Whaaat?" the policeman yelled suddenly. "Don't you know who I am and what I am? I am the owner of the house and I am to be addressed as Mister Landlord! Tie that around your finger, or else! Such a dwarf, and without manners to boot."

"Don't call me names, please," the clerk piped up.

The policeman laughed. "I certainly cut him down to size. I said dwarf and I meant it. He hands out clothes and his own stomach is rumbling. Pygmy of an official! Look at him! And he dares to open his trap at me! Humped like a marble tomcat. Stand up straight when I'm talking to you!"

He kept pouring out a stream of insults and curses he remembered from his military days.

"If you don't like it here, why don't you get off my neck?" he crowed, "Move out for all I care. I won't miss you. I could get a hundred more for every one like you. . ."

The clerk gathered his courage: "Stop shouting, please. We are here because we paid good money, not because you're doing us a favor. . ."

"Hah, hah! They gave me a miserable twenty thousand, and they think it made my fortune. Off with you, get going, you tramp, out of my sight. . ."

The clerk shrugged and slinked back to his apartment.

"What a fright you gave me!" the policeman added derisively.

"What happened?" Mrs. Syrovy asked her husband.

The clerk didn't answer. He hid his face in his hands and moaned quietly.

"Alas," he sighed after a while, "what a man I am . . . a rag, an old shoe, nothing . . . Another man would have stood up to him, but I. . . I don't know how to be rough and I don't. . . Anybody can spit in my face, and I just take it."

His wife took pity on his weakness.

"Never mind," she soothed him, "some people just don't know how to be coarse . . . you had a gentle upbringing and don't know how to face up to vulgarians. Don't let it get to you, I'll manage well enough by myself . . ."

2   The policeman kept shifting from side to side under the stifling blanket, unable to fall asleep. His mind was agitated by the thought of tenants from whom he derived no profit. The school clock chimed, the lamplighter put out the gaslight in front of the house, and the room turned dark.

"Phooey!" he spat, and got up. He gulped down a glass of water, for his mouth was parched.

"I'll think up something. . ." he mumbled, going back to bed. "I won't give up till I think of something. I'll kick them out the door, or I'll be. . ." He fell asleep at last.

And the policeman had a terrible dream:

A treasure is buried in the garden of his house. He knows about it, and looks forward to the day when he digs up the brass-studded chest full of gold ducats.

He tells himself: "I'll dig up the treasure on Thursday night, when the tenants are fast asleep."

The policeman stands on a tall hill and looks down at his garden. The moon hangs over the dead countryside like the brass basin over the barbershop. Long shadows are cast by factory smokestacks, trees, and buildings. And now he sees some figures flickering in the garden. They are his tenants, swinging picks and shovels. They laugh loudly and talk in a foreign tongue. The clerk scurries around in their midst like a grasshopper.

The policeman realizes they are digging up his treasure. He is seized by furious anger. He wants to shout — but his voice fails him. He wants to run, but he sees that his legs are missing, and in place of his right leg he's got a rubber prosthesis. He shouts: "I'll kill you, I'll kill you, I'll cut your throat!" But nobody hears him, for his voice resembles the drone of a telephone wire.

He woke up exhausted, wet with perspiration and in an ugly mood. He beat up his wife and children, and then he felt better.

3   That same night, the clerk had the following dream:

Some people come to his home. There are ten of them, no — a hundred, a whole procession. All of them have a square jaw, a mustache under their nose, and police caps. The clerk realizes that his kitchen and living room are filled by a hundred policemen, a hundred Faktors. The first Faktor mutters to himself and measures something in the room. Then he shouts: 'Atten-tion!' and thereupon the other Faktors run out and return with wheelbarrows filled with sod and manure, which they spread over the floor of his apartment. They make vegetable beds, in which they plant heads of lettuce. One of them grows so big that it pushes the clerk out the door.

On seeing this desolation, the clerk shouts: "I will invoke the protection of civil law!" But the first Faktor laughs so hard he turns red. The clerk shouts, curses, rages. But

165

nobody hears him, because he has opened the stove and is shouting his protests into the stovepipe.

Then he awoke and told his wife: "I never wanted to move to the policeman's house. That was your idea. It's all your fault."

4   At the streetcar station the policeman met a lawyer who was an acquaintance of his.

"Wheee!" the policeman whistled, and raised his finger. "What a coincidence!"

The lawyer jocularly stuck out two fingers and asked: where to, where to?

"I am going to town to buy nails; I ran out," the policeman answered politely, and thought to himself: "Lord, that fellow is loaded. I wish I had his stash."

The lawyer complained: "I've been waiting here for a quarter of an hour and nothing has come. But now that I've lit my cigar, the tram is here. Take it and finish it."

"Thanks for the cigar," the policeman said, pleased, and carefully packed it away. "My vice is cigarettes, but I'll smoke it to your health."

They boarded the streetcar and sat down facing each other. They exchanged some small talk and then the lawyer immersed himself in documents, which he pulled out of his briefcase.

"Wait a minute," the policeman thought to himself, "lawyers have all sorts of tricks up their sleeves for getting rid of tenants. I'll quietly wheedle some out of him and it won't cost me a thing. . ."

Aloud, he said: "All sorts of things go on nowadays. I know an owner of a house who has a tenant. . ."

"Hmmm," mumbled the lawyer, keeping his eye on the documents.

"It's a very interesting case, doctor," the policeman

continued. "The landlord is a fine man, but the tenant is a louse. . ."

"Hrrrrumph," the lawyer cleared his throat and covered his mouth with a handkerchief.

"The owner is trying to accommodate the tenant, but the tenant is full of spite. . ."

The lawyer ran the palm of his hand over his face.

"And so this owner comes to me, awfully dejected, and recites the sad story. Then he says: 'Mr. Faktor, do you know of any way I can get rid of this tenant? I've got another one waiting in the wings, a much better one. . .' I answered: 'There are all sorts of laws; who can make sense of them all. . . ' What sort of advice should I have given him, doctor?"

The lawyer looked up with cold eyes and said drily: "That all depends."

"Listen, doctor," the policeman added, "this fellow keeps bothering me all the time . . . I don't know what to say to him anymore . . . And that tenant of his really is a swine, and so is his wife, good God! . . . Is there any clever lawful trick that I could recommend to him?"

"Come see me at my office this afternoon and we can talk about it," said the lawyer. He put the documents back in his briefcase, touched his hat, and got off.

"Oh, that fellow is smart!" the policeman thought, impressed. "He recognized that I wanted free advice. No sir! He'd have none of it . . . 'Come see me at my office' . . . Sure, come and get fleeced. . ."

167

Chapter Twenty-six

1 "Today we'll have dinner a bit later than usual," said Mrs. Syrovy.

The clerk goes to the office, leaving his household in a state of excitement. It's laundry day, a detested day in middle-class families.

The floor is strewn with piles of laundry, wrinkled, musty, shapeless. Wicker baskets appear. An old woman arrives, wearing a faded blue apron around her sunken hips; her hair sticks out in all directions, her hands are red and cracked.

The house is in an uproar. Boiling water bubbles in a brass kettle. Steam engulfs the figure of Mrs. Syrovy as well as the woman in the faded apron.

By noon, the work was finished, for wives are careful to spare their husbands the worst travails of laundry day. When the clerk arrived for dinner, soup was steaming on the table as usual. The normal order of things was undisturbed.

The laundress sat on a footstool by the oven and drank coffee out of a blue enameled cup. Her moist face expressed the high degree of bliss which the enjoyment of coffee always bestows upon laundresses. She drank up, wiped the corners of her mouth with her thumb and index finger, and said: "The Lord bless you, madam!"

She picked up her wage and left, her clogs clip-clopping on the stairs.

"That's that," sighed Mrs. Syrovy, looking forward to some after-dinner rest.

2   But it wasn't granted her. The policeman was pacing outside, dark and angry. Greed had turned his blood into gall. He was possessed with the idea of chasing unprofitable tenants from his threshold.

All of a sudden, he started yelling: "The kettle! Just look at that kettle!"

The startled clerk put down his spoon.

"What happened? What is he yelling about now?"

Mrs. Syrovy stepped outside.

"Just come with me," the policeman raged; "come and see the condition you left the kettle in." And he rushed to the laundry room. Mrs. Syrovy followed. The clerk got up, too, to see what was going on. When they reached the laundry room, they found the policeman standing next to the kettle, red-faced as the copper. His legs were spread like a lecturer demonstrating an interesting experiment in physics. The news dealer's wife and Mrs. Soltys stood in the corner, huddled together like frightened hens.

"You call this a clean kettle?" the policeman yelled.

"What do you mean?" Mrs. Syrovy tried to defend herself. "I scrubbed the kettle for an hour with soda and sand."

"Qui-et!" the landlord boomed. "I know you. You don't fool me. You won't outsmart me. I am a kindhearted person, but I won't let my property be destroyed!"

"Who is destroying your property?" the clerk tried to object.

"I wasn't talking to you," the policeman rebuffed him. "I brought along some witnesses, so you won't be able to say I made it up." He turned to the news dealer's wife. "Is this kettle clean?"

"No," the woman squeaked, looking at the floor.

"And what do you say, Mrs. Soltys?"

"It's not in good condition," she whispered.

"So there it is!" the policeman triumphed. "Here you have impartial witnesses. If you don't put that kettle in the best of condition, I'll make short shrift of you."

He turned on his heel and stepped out of the laundry room.

"See here!" the clerk called out after him, gathering courage.

But the policeman put on his jacket, picked up a blue milk-jug, and left, muttering to himself: "I'm really fed up!"

3   "How could you say that the kettle wasn't clean?" Mrs. Syrovy reproached her fellow tenants.

"Please, Mrs. Syrovy, don't be angry. . ." Mrs. Soltys said in a pleading voice. "We know very well there's nothing wrong with the kettle. But what were we to do? He came barging in: You must bear witness. You know what he's like. He's capable of anything. I fear him like the devil. He'll bring disaster down on all of us. . ."

The news dealer's wife started to cry.

"A person wants to get along with everybody," she sobbed, "and it can't be done. Holy Mother in heaven, what I have to put up with is beyond words . . . I bow down to the ground before him. Just to keep from losing the roof over my head. He never gave us the contract he promised us. He says: We'll see. And so we find ourselves without any protection, completely at his mercy."

"He has it in for us," moaned Mrs. Syrovy, "and yet we try so hard . . . We wouldn't put a blade of grass in his way."

"It's all in vain," said the news dealer's wife. "He wants to get you out of the house, and so all your efforts are useless. Day after day he comes after me and asks: What news? Any problem with the Syrovys? No shouting or quarrels between you? Why not? Why aren't there any disputes? Are you by any chance siding against me? Be careful! Somebody told him that tenants who don't get along with others can be evicted from their apartment. That's why he's trying to get us squabbling with each other. But I am not the quarreling type . . . Let him leave me in peace. I wash his laundry and clean up for him for nothing, just to be left alone . . . I'll do something awful to myself, if he doesn't stop it. . ." she lamented.

"We're all in a fine pickle," mumbled the clerk.

4   Night fell on the suburb. All creatures slept, only the policeman was awake. Carefully he wrote and drew lines on a sheet of paper. When he finished his work, his hand held a neat table divided into regular sections. It had the title:

> SCHEDULE FOR WASHING OF LAUNDRY

The table divided the month into regular segments of time; and each segment signified a day when individual tenants were allowed to wash laundry.

To the table was appended an

> EXPLANATION

which stated:

> If a particular day falls on a holiday,
> washday will be moved up to the following day.

And further:

171

Chapter Twenty-seven

1 The month of September arrived. The days turned transparent and tenderly melancholy. The shrubs and trees on the slopes thinned out; and in the parks dead leaves rustled under pedestrians' feet. In the fields, smoke from campfires rose to the clean, steely sky, and amid loud merriment young people flew paper kites. The sun still had some strength; but one could feel the end of summer approaching.

In the policeman's garden, the apple ripened. One day the landlord picked off the fruit, which was yellow with red stripes. He wrapped the apple in a kerchief and carried it home as carefully as if it was a precious balm. He kept it on the window sill for a while and enjoyed looking at it. But at last he concluded that fruit was the kind of property the value of which is realized only in the act of consumption.

So he gathered his family, divided the apple into four parts, since the family consisted of four members, and said with deep emotion: "Here is the first apple from my garden. Eat it. That apple grew from my sapling, which I planted in my soil. Nobody else may eat of this apple, only I myself, and then you, after I give it to you. Eat it and remember that I am the son of poor parents, and it is only thanks to my diligence and foresight that I now own a house and a garden. Whatever lives on my soil is under my dominion. Whoever desecrates my property will feel my anger."

Thereupon the family silently consumed the apple, completely immersed in the solemnity of the moment.

2   Mrs. Syrovy was in Mr. Mejstrik's store, doing the marketing for her household. Next to her stood a woman in a kerchief, who had completed her purchase but hesitated to leave, because her visit to the grocer gave her an opportunity to be among people. She used the occasion to start a conversation with Mrs. Syrovy.

She asked: "You live in the Faktors' house?"

The grocer perked up his ears and called out: "Anything else I can serve you with? Chicory? Or coffee? French, Viennese, special mix, I carry them all."

"No thanks," answered the woman. "So you live at the policeman's? I must say I don't envy you. . ."

"Fresh spice, anise, pepper," the grocer broke in nervously, "perhaps you've run out. . .?"

"I have enough spices," said the woman. "He's quite a case, that policeman of yours. What a tight-wad. . ."

"I have scrubbing-brushes, genuine bristle hairbrushes, kindly let me show you. . ." shouted the grocer.

"I don't need any . . . Oh, that Faktor is notorious . . . Once he. . ."

"Slippers, known as mikados," the grocer screamed in desperation; "they're extremely useful, very practical around the house. I have them in stock at a big reduction."

"What do I need slippers for . . . I have my own, I can't even wear them out. That fellow Faktor is in hot water with the police department, because during the war he took bribes to wink at profiteers. . ."

"Lady!" moaned Mr. Mejstrik. "Stock up on semolina . . . Lentils, peas, millet, wood alcohol. . ."

"Another time. That's how the policeman got the wherewithal to build himself a house. . ."

"Dear lady! Haven't you forgotten something? You'll get home and tell yourself: How silly of me, I wanted to get some vinegar. . ."

"Oh no! I never forget anything. Now he throws his weight around and acts as if he owned the town. And he's oppressive to everybody. . ."

The grocer suddenly launched into frenzied singing:

> She stood by the door, as fresh as a rose,
> A maid with a wreath on her head.
> Then she stepped out, the wind caught the wreath,
> And her carefree young days are dead. . .

he sang, skipping about like a man possessed.

"You seem unusually merry today, Mr. Mejstrik," the woman remarked suspiciously.

"I am! I am!" the grocer exclaimed. "And why shouldn't I be merry, when I am so young and handsome. Oh, I know so many songs, such beautiful songs, you'd be amazed. The next time you come, I'll sing some of them for you, such as the one about the murder on Luzice Street. You know it? Listen: 'Anna Behm on Luzice Street, she looks so inviting, she looks so sweet, playing the cello, in the bordello. . .'"

"Leave me alone with that nonsense," the woman shouted with contempt, "I'm not much for songs. . ."

And she left, indicating with a gesture to Mrs. Syrovy that the grocer must have had one too many.

174

When the grocer found himself alone, he wiped the perspiration from his forehead and groaned: "Damn women! They're always after that policeman. Can't they gab about him somewhere else? They'll get me in hot water, and it won't be my fault..."

3   It is written that no one escapes his fate. In the morning, the grocer was bringing the policeman's wife a pot of milk, as was his daily duty. In the yard of the house his eyes saw the following drama:

He saw the occupants of the house gathered in a circle. In the middle of the ring stood two women with arms akimbo and disheveled hair. They were piercing each other with ferocious looks.

"You call yourself Madame Engineer? You call yourself a landlady?" screamed the policeman's wife. "In my eyes you're the pit of the pits!"

Her opponent, Mrs. Mandaus, was no slouch when it came to using her mouth. She was the policeman's landlady, a wild old woman steeled by frequent quarrels with the tenants of her house on Harant Street. Though she had a meager body and the hooked nose of an owl, she would throw herself into disputes with enormous élan, battling over her supremacy against a whole houseful of dissatisfied tenants.

"And you call yourself the wife of a policeman?" she answered. "You are supposed to keep order in the house, and instead you instigate trouble and cause mischief!"

"*I* cause mischief?" the policeman's wife raised her voice a whole fifth. "I dare you to say that again!"

"*You* cause mischief," the landlady repeated, her eyes seeking moral support among the audience. "Instead of teaching your urchins good manners, you incite them to spit on my window..."

"Don't you dare call my children urchins," shrieked the policeman's wife, "you. . . you. . ."

"You what? What were you going to call me?" the landlady asked threateningly.

"You know perfectly well," answered the policeman's wife.

"What do I know perfectly well?" asked the landlady.

"You are notorious, everybody will agree with me," and the policeman's wife looked for support from the bystanders. But the gathering was apathetic, for neither the landlady nor the policeman's wife enjoyed any popularity in the house.

The battle grew hotter. Passions were ignited.

"You. . . you. . ." the landlady breathed heavily, "you frumpy frump you . . . phooey, phooey!"

"How dare you!" screamed the policeman's wife. "You . . . You call yourself Madame Engineer, but in reality you're a hawker from the flea market. You used to peddle pots and pans on Kampa Island. We know all about you. You don't fool us one bit. We'll cut you down to size. . ."

"This is unheard of!" The landlady was horrified. "Such a low-down person dares to. . . Woman! Don't push me too far. . .! Or I'll lose my temper . . . I am not so vulgar as to bother with you . . . you old goosebrain. . ."

"What? You called me a goosebrain? Very well. Mr. Mejstrik, you are a witness!"

"You called me a hawker from the flea-market. Mr. Mejstrik is a witness."

"You're a witness!"

"You're a witness!"

Both rivals began to touch Mr. Mejstrik with their index fingers like children playing 'you're it.'

The poor grocer's brain was reeling.

"I. . ." he mumbled "I only brought the milk. . ."

"You're a witness that she called me a goosebrain," the policeman's wife squealed.

"You're my witness that she insulted me," crowed the landlady.

"I brought some milk. . ." mumbled Mr. Mejstrik, "excellent milk, highest quality, I always have fresh goods, just visit my store. . ."

At that point, the policeman was returning from duty. Seeing the hubbub, his domineering instincts came to the fore.

"Disperse!" he ordered. "Keep moving! Quickly, quickly, or you'll come with me."

A subdued murmur rippled through the gathering and people dispersed, avidly discussing the events.

"Punish your wife," croaked the landlady. "Arrest her, if you have a grain of fairness in you. For she is the cause of everything."

"Quiet!" the policeman bellowed. "I don't want to hear another word. Everybody go home. Mrs. Mandaus, I ask you in the name of the law to return to your abode!"

"Don't you call me Mrs. Mandaus," the wild old woman protested; "I am your landlady. And if you don't like it, move out. That will be fine with me."

"Quiet! How dare you talk that way? I have a mind to arrest you for interference with official duty! Go home in opposite directions, Anastazie to the left, Mrs. Mandaus to the right. . ."

"Don't you act so high and mighty. In this house you have no business giving orders, for I am the landlady and you're just a tenant. This woman dared to call me bad names. I am going to take you to court. . ."

"Hah, hah! Do that, by all means, if you think it will do you any good. Be my guest. You see, I know my way around the courthouse. I will introduce circumstances before the court showing that you are illegally exerting pressure on us to move out. And the judge will throw the book at you for contempt of the rights of tenants. . ."

"Excuse me," broke in a young man with a rat-like face, "allow me to explain that Mrs. Mandaus is the victim of a wrong, because your wife declared that she wasn't Madame Engineer but a peddler . . . If you're at all impartial, you have to judge her fairly, because it is generally known that the deceased husband of Mrs. Mandaus was an engineer, and thus. . ."

"Did I ask for your opinion?" the policeman burst out, casting a crushing glance at the rat-faced youth. "I didn't ask you, so mind your own business. . ."

"That's my future son-in-law," Mrs. Mandaus piped up, "and he therefore has a right to come to my defense. People can't even speak up anymore."

"Son-in-law, that's a good one," the policeman's wife laughed with a smirk. "There's plenty of them on every corner . . . if a girl has no shame, she can have fifty of them. . ."

"What do you mean by that?" shrieked Mrs. Mandaus. "I'm going to. . . Mr. Mejstrik is a witness that you besmirched my daughter's honor. . ."

"Mr. Mejstrik is my witness and he'll tell the court plenty. . ."

"Witness?" Mr. Mejstrik groaned. "I know nothing . . . I brought the milk . . . I was just standing here . . . I am an old man and I don't understand what everyone's talking about. . ."

"We'll meet in the courthouse!" the landlady shouted.

"My pleasure," the policeman's wife bowed sarcastically.

"Will you all be quiet!" shouted the policeman.

"Let's go home, Mrs. Mandaus," the rat-faced youth

said, dragging the landlady by her skirt. "The truth will come out in court, and it will be obvious who is the public nuisance. . ."

4   "Oh, good Lord in heaven. . ." the grocer moaned on his way home. "Now you're really in hot water, Mejstrik . . . You'll be a witness before the court, they say. They didn't even ask whether I was willing or not . . . What sort of a witness am I, for dear Jesus' sake! So help me, I know nothing. Speak to me like angels, speak to me like devils, I haven't heard anything nor seen anything, because I have a foolish old noggin . . . Honorable Court, of course I want to tell the whole truth . . . but if you want to get the facts, call somebody else, there were plenty of people around. Thick as flies, if I may express myself that way. What do you want with an old codger like me. Get some young fellow and he'll tell you short and sweet how everything happened. . .

"Some people have a nimble tongue, they have such a gift of speech that sparks fly out of their mouth . . . I don't know how to talk . . . my eyes are weak and my ears don't hear, for I am going on seventy, which as the Honorable Court knows is quite an age.

"They say you're a witness. What kind of witness, for heaven's sake? I have a store . . . I make a living as the good Lord directs. I give everybody good service. Nobody can say a word against me. Does the Honorable Court require shoelaces? I am at your service. Does the Honorable Court want shoe polish, candles, soap? Certainly . . . Also jam, soda, sugar, chicory, everything in stock. Whips, pen holders, cherry pipes, whatever the Honorable Court needs. It takes a heap of worry, running such a business. I can't afford to think about anything else . . . I can't leave my store, that would ruin me . . . I beg the Honorable Court to excuse me from appearing as a witness, for I am not qualified . . . I am a tradesman and not a witness. I have to get along with everybody. You say the wrong word and you lose a customer . . . I'll say it straight out: Everyone, including the Honorable Court to boot, can kiss my behind. So, there you have it. . .!"

He came home and said plaintively to his wife: "Ah, Majdalena, a great disaster has struck our old heads. I'm faint and I feel as weak as a fly. . ."

He lay down. His wife brewed him some herbal tea.

Chapter Twenty-eight

1   He kept hoping that he wouldn't be called. Perhaps they'll just shrug it off, why bother with an old codger like me. After all, I don't even know what it's about. Perhaps they'll forget. There are such cases. Damned nuisance. This is all I needed.

In vain. One day the postman brought an official letter. With a practiced movement, the postman tore off the receipt and requested the addressee to endorse it. The grocer sighed: "This means trouble," and signed it in his clumsy, unsteady handwriting.

The notice specified that Mr. Mejstrik was to present himself before the district court, room so and so, at ten o'clock in order to testify in the case of Faktor versus Mandaus. "In the event you fail to comply, a warrant will be issued for your arrest," the court warned.

"That's all I need," Mr. Mejstrik muttered gloomily: "to be led across the street with a bayonet at my back, like a criminal. That would be a great recommendation for my business . . . But I'll go quietly. They don't have to threaten me. I'm an honest man. Anyone will tell you. I've lived in the same place for forty years. My taxes are in order, so kindly desist from shooting off your trap at me. . ."

He dressed as neatly as if going to a funeral. He felt weak in the knees. His intestines sang a desperate melody as he set out on his way. His wife saw him off to the door and called out after him: "Tell them that you don't know anything and that we are about to sell the store. We'll move in with our son at Vodnany. By all means tell them, so that they realize what's what."

Mr. Mejstrik answered: "You bet I'll tell them, and a lot else besides."

When he got on the streetcar, he remarked to the conductor punching his ticket: "These days you need a head as big as mattress to have room for all your worries."

"That's right, Mr. Mejstrik," the streetcar man agreed.

2   The somber hallway of the district court teems with people. Portly officials with pipes in their mouth open and close doors. Occasionally a girl scurries by with documents in her arms; she munches a sandwich on the run. A convict in overalls sweeps the floor. People sit on benches. A country bumpkin with sunken temples. A man with a hat pulled over his eyes. A girl in a green sweater. All of them have the preoccupied expression typical of railway travelers.

Mr. Mejstrik paces back and forth, feeling lost. If only they'd call him already. He'd quietly tell them everything, and they'd appreciate his effort. The main thing is not to say anything he might regret later.

He steps up to a window with a milky pane thickly covered with the kind of obscene drawings seen in public places. Someone's hand felt itself called upon to state that "dance is rhythmic nonsense." The author of this thought signed his name and dutifully added the date. A dissatisfied critic declared that "whoever wrote this is an idiot." Another author proclaimed that he had sat in this building from the fifteenth of June to the fourth of September. "You can call me a thief," he wrote, "but you're thieves yourselves. And the biggest thief of all is prison superintendent Punata. . ."

Mr. Mejstrik turns away and looks at the door of the courtroom, from which he can hear loud shouting.

3   The judge, a handsome, white-haired old man, sits behind a crucifix, his head resting on his palm. The gloomy-faced recorder gazes out the window into the street, scratching his greasy hair with a penholder.

In the middle of the room, in an area marked by a divider, the two parties are disputing. The policeman's wife and Mrs. Mandaus are continuing the discussion begun the other day in the yard. The wild old woman is supported on one side by the rat-faced youth and on the other by her daughter, a girl with a pointy nose. The policeman's wife stands with her arms akimbo and from her lips pours a stream of words like a mountain torrent. Her husband is by her side, trying to decide: "Should I intervene — or shouldn't I intervene?"

The judge wakes up from his ruminations and rises to his feet. His long years of experience have taught him that before any court case begins, it is a good idea to let the quarreling parties talk themselves out. He knows that they'll be more open to compromise then.

With his hands crossed behind him, he paces deliberately between the door and the window and, in a quiet, moving voice, utters his usual words of wisdom: "Well, well . . . It's not nice to see two intelligent women insulting one another. True, all of us are a bit nervous, that's not surprising in these postwar days. Somebody says something without meaning any harm. Shake hands and make up. For the sake of good will in the house. . ."

"Make up? Never!" shouts the wild woman.

"Shake hands with that?" shrieks the policeman's wife. "Honorable judge, I demand that she be thrown in jail for her vileness!"

Once again a hubbub breaks out, in which the pleas of the judge are completely lost.

"Oh, my God," moans the wild old woman, "I'm about to faint. . ."

"Mother!" exclaims the girl with the pointy nose.

"Dear lady, let me help you. . ." shouts the rat-faced man.

"Gentlemen . . ." the judge turns imploringly to the two lawyers. But the lawyer with the cold eyes shrugs his shoulders, and his opponent stretches out his arms as a sign that nothing can be done.

When the noisy commotion calmed down somewhat, the judge asked: "Tell me, Mrs. Mandaus, why did you file two complaints? Who wrote the other one for you?"

"I did," the rat-faced youth announced proudly and stepped forward.

"But why?"

"Just because. . . because a lawyer never takes as much care as one's own family."

"Why do you stick your nose into things you know nothing about? Don't you realize that your complaint gives rise to a new insult? You accuse Mrs. Faktor of having written an anonymous letter, where did I put it, ah, here it is . . . 'You old goosebrain, you lay around all day with your dog and your daughter with her boyfriend who doesn't leave her for an instant even when she goes to the . . .' Phooey! I can't even read this swill . . . How can you maintain that these are expressions 'constantly coming out of Mrs. Faktor's mouth.' "

"Please, your Honor, I can call the whole street as witness that everything is the God's truth. . ."

"My daughter is pure. . ." shouts the wild old woman.

"Your honor, I requested that an investigating official come and check the facts on the spot," said the rat-faced man. "They don't like the way our dog smells, but imagine the smell of those thirty rabbits of theirs. . ."

At this point the policeman cleared his throat and winked at the judge like a high-placed personage used to dealing with his equals. He began: "Most honorable judge! Legally speaking, it is evident that the original circumstances. . ."

He had evidently prepared a lengthy address. But the white-haired judge grasped the sides of his head and groaned: "What's going on? What's the meaning of this?"

"In view of the facts," the rat-faced youth took the floor again, "why don't you ask Mr. Faktor what he was doing in our cellar on the fourteenth of June . . . I watched through the window, but I was afraid of getting hit over the head, because the safety situation. . ."

"Out!" shouted the judge. "If you don't want to make peace, very well. The case will begin. The two parties will stay here and everyone else will leave the room. Well, how about it?" he turned to the rat-faced young man.

"Let's go, Blazenka" he said to his fiancée.

"Alas, my children!" the wild old woman exclaimed. "You are leaving me and I am at death's door. . ."

"Mom is fainting," moaned the girl with the pointy nose.

"Let's go, Blazenka . . . we'll leave our case in the hands of justice . . . it will become clear who said 'that's what one can expect from your kind,' and she said 'kind' in such a way that everybody. . ."

"Get out this instant!" the white-haired judge shouted. "And what about you?" He turned to the policeman. "What are you waiting for?"

"Me?" asked the policeman, surprised that the judge failed to consider him a person in a position of authority, "I want to be by the side of my wife . . . I'm ready to explain various circumstances . . . to shed sharp light on the conditions in the house. . ."

"Leave the room at once," the judge said drily.

Mumbling "I marvel at this," the policeman left the courtroom.

4   "Call the witness!" the judge ordered.

The recorder opened the door and called out: "Mr. Mejstrik!"

Mr. Mejstrik felt a pang in his stomach, as if he had swallowed a knotted rope.

"Here, over here." The scribe took Mr. Mejstrik by the shoulder and stood him up in front of the crucifix.

"You are Mr. Mejstrik?" asked the judge.

"Well then, Mr. Mejstrik . . . on the fourth of September a disturbance allegedly occurred in the yard of number 27 Harant Street. What can you tell us about that? You must speak the truth, otherwise you'll be punished."

"I always tell the truth," mumbled the witness, wiping the perspiration from his forehead.

"So what happened?"

"What happened . . . Take the milk, says my wife, to the Faktors' . . . All right, I says, but you stay in the store and take care of the customers. I carry the pot of milk . . . Sometimes they order a liter, sometimes half a liter, all according . . . So then I bring them the milk. . ."

"Just a moment. You entered the yard and you heard shouting. Mrs. Mandaus was quarreling with Mrs. Faktor. And what happened then?"

"What happened . . . I brought the milk, and they were talking . . . Talking very loud. . ."

"Talking? Some talk. They were yelling at each other and calling each other names. What kind of names?"

"If you please, your Honor, I don't know . . . I came there in the middle. . ."

"Did you hear Mrs. Faktor say to Mrs. Mandaus 'you are a hawker from the flea-market'?"

"And a year ago she called me 'you old goat,' " the wild woman broke in. "She was standing by the compost heap and yelling those words at the top of her lungs. . ."

"Quiet! Witness, did you hear the expression 'hawker from the flea-market'?"

"No sir, I didn't."

"How come? Are you deaf?"

"Not exactly."

"All right, then . . . And did you hear Mrs. Mandaus call Mrs. Faktor 'you old goosebrain'?"

"I can't oblige."

"Good Lord, man!" the judge shouted angrily. "Where were you standing, that you didn't hear a word?"

"I was standing by the pot of milk. I put it down next to me and looked around. . ."

"Surely you can't tell me you heard nothing?"

"I heard and I didn't. There were voices, but I didn't pay attention. . ."

"Be careful! A witness mustn't hide anything. There is heavy punishment for that. . ."

"Your Honor, I would gladly help," the witness mumbled. "I'm not hiding anything . . . but I have such a wooden old head. . ."

"So you claim you know nothing?" the judge asked threateningly.

"I know and I don't."

"What do you know?"

"What should I know? I say something, there's trouble— I say nothing, there's also trouble. If you please, your Honor, I'm not much of a talker. It's best not to talk to me at all. My wife always says: 'What an old fool you are,' and it's true. There's no way of pleasing people. You can't take sides. I'm glad to serve any customer, providing they act fair. My wife asked me to announce that we're selling our business."

"What's that?" groaned the judge.

"Our store. We're selling out. It's not worth the trouble. We went through enough all these years. We're going to move to Vodnany, we have a son there, he's a manager."

"Ahh!" the judge sighed and wiped his forehead with his hand.

He suddenly turned red, struck the table with his fist, and thundered at the witness: "Get out, get out of my sight! Before I commit an act of slander against you!"

"That's right, your Honor," the grocer said happily, "no point in wasting your breath on my wooden head. Someone like me doesn't belong in a court, he ought to stay at home. I beg to take my leave, your Honor. . ."

And blissfully he slipped out the door like a mouse.

"And now," the judge spat out in a fury, "you'll make peace or I'll lock up the both of you!"

Once again, commotion broke out in the courtroom. There was weeping, moaning, and groaning. It took a long time before the judge and the two lawyers managed to calm the disputing women. The recorder wrote up the agreement and both sides signed it.

"And now," the judge declared ceremoniously, "you mustn't pay any attention to one another, understand?"

"Why should I pay attention?" said Mrs. Mandaus. "I'm happy to get her out of my sight."

"I wouldn't touch her with a long stick," said the policeman's wife.

The rat-faced youth and the girl with the pointy nose led Mrs. Mandaus out the door.

In the hall, the policeman said to the rat-faced youth:
"You find my rabbits too smelly for you, Mr. Zpevak?
Very well. I'll show you what it means to slander my
rabbits. . ."

Chapter Twenty-nine

1   "Another load off my back," the judge said
with satisfaction.

The hum of silence filled the courtroom. The policeman
paced the hall, waiting for his lawyer.

The white-haired judge put the documents in a file and
got ready to leave. Then he paused for a moment, lost in
thought, and absentmindedly lay the documents back on
the table.

"Oh, my dear gentlemen. . ." he sighed and turned to
the lawyers, who were deeply absorbed in making notes.

He folded his hands under his robe, frowned, and
continued: "For thirty years, gentlemen, I've been serving
the district court . . . That's something! For thirty years I've
been listening to the shouting, weeping, and tirades of
quarreling people . . . Day after day, like a machine, I
launch into my speech about the need for human toler-
ance. . ."

The policeman's lawyer heaved a sigh in response.

"And all in vain . . . Thirty years! There is no salvation
for me. I am chained to this place by an evil spell. . ."

"Well," answered Mrs. Mandaus' lawyer, stroking his

bald pate, "it's no fun, I grant you . . . Anyone who ever had occasion to listen to my client, even just once, is fed up with her up to here. She is certainly a certified old pest."

"Never mind your old biddy, my dear colleague," his opponent remarked; "she's an angel compared to that Faktor sourpuss of mine . . . Believe me!"

"I can see, dear colleague, that you don't know Mrs. Mandaus . . . That lady has already sued her way out of two houses, and legal expenses will shortly eat up the third. . ."

"Still, you can't blame her when she has such tenants as my honorable client. Sweet Jesus. . .!"

"That's all well and good, my dear colleague. But you would have to be privy to the history of Mrs. Mandaus to appreciate all her fine qualities. That poor, defenseless widow served eighteen months in jail for bribing someone to bear false witness. That was during the time when she owned the Seven Angels building in Vinohrady. Her specialty consisted of dragging her tenants into endless lawsuits. She employed people whom she paid to act as witnesses. That's how she got rid of tenants. Those were the days . . . The judge here knows about those cases. . ."

The white-haired judge waved his arm in a gesture of resignation.

"I've often thought about ways to achieve better relations between landlords and tenants," he began. "Always the same story. Children, poultry, domestic animals; soiling the stairs, noise in the house, wasting water; the tenants slander the landlord, the tenants don't respect the landlord, the landlord believes he's cursed with the worst tenants. Endless yelling and complaining. In reality the conflict derives from the fact that people use someone else's property. It's as if landlords and tenants were being forced to eat from a common plate . . . Ownership is grafted upon human individuality. And so when strangers occupy the landlord's house, he feels as if they were living in his innards. I often come to the conclusion that buildings occupied by several families should be public property. But I don't really understand it; I'm too old. Pardon a foolish old man. . ."

The bald lawyer laughed.

"Sometimes one must really marvel," he said, "at the ideas people come up with when they plot to deprive someone of money without breaking the law. I had one such client. In his house lived a tradesman who wanted to fix up a workshop. The landlord gave him permission, provided he made the alterations at his own expense. Fine. The tradesman called a contractor, who built him the workshop. When the job was finished, he found out that he had no access to the workshop. He'd have to cross the yard, but the landlord prohibited him from doing that, since use of the yard was not part of his contract. 'I'll let you walk across the yard,' the landlord said, 'if you fix it up nicely.'

Fine. The tenant paved the yard and raised it by fifty centimeters. When it was done, the landlord raised the tenant's rent. 'You can't expect to use such a beautiful workshop and yard for the original rent. That wouldn't be fair to me.' The tenant agreed to the rent increase. Shortly thereafter, the landlord sold the house to the contractor who had constructed the workshop. The new landlord kicked the tradesman out, because he needed the workshop for his garage. . ."

"That reminds me of another case," said the lawyer with the cold eyes. "A certain man wanted to build a house but didn't have the money. He bought a building lot on credit. He then found some tenants who gave him a down payment for construction. He dug the foundations. Then he stopped. The tenants were impatient and complained. The fellow returned their money, but of course without interest. He found other tenants and built the walls. Again he stopped. History repeated itself. With the money of the new tenants he finished the building, but he took his time with the inside. He got some more tenants, who had to come up with a down payment and also had to pay high rents. Today the man has both a house and money. A clever fellow, very practical. . ."

"That is standard practice nowadays," the bald lawyer remarked sarcastically. "That is normal operating procedure for today's builders. But I want to tell you something else. It's a very amusing story. A fellow built himself a house, in which he had an empty room that he rented to an unmarried man for five thousand crowns annually. The tenant gave him the money. Fine. A month later the landlord calls the tenant and says: My good man! I need that room for a relative. If you move out, I'll give you two thousand back. The tenant refused to move. The landlord sued him for bodily assault, for he knew that raising one's hand against a landlord is grounds for eviction."

2   The policeman suddenly entered the courtroom and heard the last few words.

"Oh ho!" he rejoiced. "Raising one's hand against a landlord is grounds for eviction! Very interesting! And my lawyer didn't say a word to me about it, the scoundrel. He took my money, though. To hell with him. . ."

". . . grounds for eviction," continued the bald-headed lawyer. "He always had his people who testified that the tenant had committed violence against him. And so he kept taking on tenants and evicting them. And lived it up.

Until in the end everything went wrong. Now he travels around selling picture postcards."

"Yes. . ." sighed the lawyer with the cold eyes, "one would much rather represent pirates than that sort." He turned to the policeman and said: "Just a moment, Mr. Faktor, I'm almost ready."

But the policeman was in no hurry. His unspoken words were burning on his tongue like hot coals. He wanted to recite the speech which the judge had kept him from delivering during the court session.

He stepped up to the judge's podium and said: "Honorable Court! I wished to explain the circumstances. . ."

"Go on, officer," the judge encouraged him indulgently. He was in a kindly mood, because he had succeeded in putting a conciliatory end to a nasty case.

"I am a good-natured person by nature," the policeman began. "I try to get along with everyone, in peace. A person tries to be considerate, and they repay him with ingratitude. Give the other fellow his due, try to help out the other fellow, that's my motto. . ."

"Quite right," the judge praised him.

The policeman grew animated.

"But tenants are such a low-down bunch, it's unbelievable. A landlord wracks his brain thinking how to make their stay in his house more pleasant. But does he get any gratitude? No sir! All they think about is how to commit some nuisance. They plan all kinds of plots behind the landlord's back and ruin the landlord's sleep. Kindly believe me that they destroy property, they have no respect for landlords, and they disturb the peace. . ."

"You are right," remarked the judge, "but since you see everything so clearly, why don't you convince your wife to be on good terms with her landlord and stop making trouble?"

The policeman was taken aback. He suddenly realized that he was a tenant himself. He said to himself: "Watch out!"

"I request permission to explain everything . . . Of course, there are tenants and there are tenants. Some hunker down and are as quiet as a mouse, extra careful not to give the landlord any reason to complain. But some landlords have no gratitude. Like ours . . . They say she is a harridan. I don't know about that. I don't use such words. All I know is that she is a lawless woman. I try to warn her for her own sake. 'Mrs. Mandaus,' I command, 'don't stand around in the yard, and pay no attention to the tenants. We can't have shouting and quarrels. Stay in your apartment to prevent trouble. . .' But do you think she listens to me? No sir! She just keeps shooting off her trap, if you'll excuse the expression. So one thing leads to another . . . Our landlady doesn't know the meaning of morality if she allows her daughter to carry on with that young man. . ."

"All right, very well. . ." the judge lifted his hand.

"Let's go, Mr. Faktor," the lawyer said, rising.

But the policeman was greatly moved by his own mellifluous speech. He felt like elaborating on it.

"I am a landlord myself," he said warmly, "but not the sort of landlord who marries into property or inherits it or steals it. I made myself a landlord. And my house is the most beautiful of all. When you're in the neighborhood, stop by. I'll give you a rose from my garden. Gladly. I like to see people happy. . ."

The judge picked up his papers and was about to leave. The policeman, too, was ready to go. But when he reached the door, he turned around and added: "If you please, your Honor, I won two silver medals as a wrestling champion. You can check on it. I am speaking the truth. . ."

3   In the hall, he said to his lawyer in a mysterious voice: "I have an alibi against him."

"What alibi?" asked the surprised lawyer.

"Such a powerful alibi that I only need to mention it and he'll go flying out of my house one, two, three."

"Who?"

"That tenant of mine. You remember, I told you in the streetcar. . ."

"But weren't you referring to some other landlord?"

"That's true, yes. But I have very similar problems with a tenant of mine. That seems to be the general situation."

"Are you talking about some evidence on the basis of which your tenant could be evicted?"

"Yes, that's it."

The lawyer examined his fingernails and then said: "Come see me this afternoon in my office. This is neither the time nor the place to deal with such matters." And he held out two fingers as a parting gesture.

The policeman gazed after the lawyer and grunted angrily: "No visit in no office. I know how much that would cost. I'll handle this matter myself, in a proper, legal way. . ."

4   "Raising a hand against a landlord is grounds for eviction." That sentence came to nest in his brain.

"Raising a hand . . . That would be fine. But that scoundrel won't raise his hand against me. . ." The policeman ground his teeth. "Such a stunted pygmy, how would he dare? Why, he's just a dwarf . . . a runty runt. . ."

Striding home, he cursed the clerk for his physical weakness and timidity. He felt the need to stop by at the tavern, to chase away his gloomy thoughts.

He came home at night, flushed and in high spirits. He

gathered the family around him and said: "Now we'll give that old bag a performance in honor of our reconciliation."

Thereupon the policeman's wife picked up a tin kettle and started beating it with a soup ladle. Both children armed themselves with brooms and pounded the floor in rhythm. The policeman puffed out his cheeks and proceeded to blow shrill bursts on his bugle. It was a hellish concert that threw the whole house into an uproar.

"Oh Lord. . ." sighed the wild old lady, "they're starting up again. I'll go mad from it all." She opened the door and called out into the hall: "Are you going to stop that or not?"

This was answered by a single resounding word from the policeman.

And the concert continued deep into the night.

Chapter Thirty

1   The piece of land measuring six thousand one hundred and twenty square meters came under a dark cloud. The house on the outskirts of the city turned into a jail, surrounded by crenelated battlements. The Syrovys now spent their time sitting glumly in the kitchen, afraid to leave their apartment whenever they suspected the landlord's presence in the garden. The policeman couldn't bear the sight of these tenants. He couldn't forgive them for their unwillingness to move out, thus depriving him of profit. The thought of getting rid of the Syrovys preoccupied his every moment, and he trudged after this thought in a circle, like a horse hitched to a whim-gin.

When coming across the couple, the policeman would burst into shrill insults and curses. And he didn't mind that his voice resounded through the entire street. The Syrovys were isolated. The inhabitants of the neighborhood were afraid to show them any sympathy.

Only the shoemaker from across the street sided with the beleaguered tenants. He sat by the window busily working, yet at the same time watching what went on outside. He had an unruly instinct for helping the persecuted.

"Madam," he said to Mrs. Syrovy, "those shoes want new soles. The heels, too, are worn. I'll have them for you by Sunday, you can depend on it. And that landlord of yours, that bastard of a flatfoot, I'll let him have it as soon as he comes within range. I'll teach him not to harass decent citizens. . ."

"Careful, Supita!" his wife admonished. "What a way to talk! You'll get in trouble that way."

"Be quiet," the shoemaker responded. "I'm not afraid of anything. I can't stand to look at injustice. I've been jailed and persecuted myself. I'll tell everybody what I think straight out. Good people are being persecuted, and I have to give that dirty scoundrel a piece of my mind. That woman, his wife, is no better. One time I brought them some shoes and caught the policeman slapping his wife. I got angry and said: 'Is this any way, Mr. Faktor, to treat a woman?' — And he: 'Mind your own business, this has nothing to do with you. My wife belongs to me and I can do with her as I please.' — 'No sir!' I said. 'A woman is nobody's property, a woman has equal rights.'

'Get the hell out,' he answered, 'before I put you under arrest.' 'You have nothing to arrest me for, I haven't done anything.' — And at that point she herself turned on me: 'Mind your business,' she says to me. — 'Very well, if that's how you want it, I won't intervene any further.'"

"One day you'll be sorry that you have such a brass mouth," warned the shoemaker's wife.

2   "Is *he* around?"

"I haven't seen him," his wife answered, "perhaps he's on duty."

"I'd like to step outside for a bit," the clerk said mournfully. "It's like being in jail here. . ."

"You go right ahead and get some air. We have a perfect right to do that. *He* can't prevent us. After all, we rented an apartment with fresh air. . ."

The clerk went out on the terrace.

In the garden, locked by a padlock, the last flowers were blooming. Brightly colored dahlias and asters were covered with gray frost. Sunflowers spread out their yellow targets.

Decay and dissolution were in the autumnal air. With suspicion in his heart, the clerk gazed at the last glories of the fading summer. It seemed to him that the sunflowers bloomed only because the policeman so ordered it; the dahlias were yellow, red, and orange because those were the policeman's orders. Rain fell on the six thousand one hundred and twenty square meters of earth only when the policeman's plants required it. All of nature demarcated by this plot of land was subject to the policeman; floating over everything was an absent policeman without whose will not a single dry leaf dropped from a branch.

Full of gloomy thoughts he straggled into the yard. The rabbits, hearing steps, scurried around in their hutches and stared at the clerk with their big eyes. He didn't like the way they wiggled their noses.

"Don't laugh at me," he growled. "There's nothing to laugh at . . . You belong to the policeman, too; he can cut your throats any time he feels like it. . ."

A scraggly-necked hen stepped up and cast a fixed eye at the clerk.

The clerk became angry.

"What are you gaping at, you police biddy?" he shouted. "Shoo — beat it! Have you been sent to spy on me?"

The frightened hen ran off amid noisy cackling.

Suddenly a shiver ran through the clerk. He turned; behind him stood the policeman, mighty and terrible. In silent fury, he stared the clerk right in the eye.

"Well?" he said after a few moments. "Don't you know your manners?"

The clerk cowered and tried to slink away.

The policeman stopped him.

"Don't you know how to greet your landlord?" he rasped. "I've long been noticing that you've stopped greeting me. That must be some sort of new vogue, not greeting one's landlord. If you don't like it here, move out . . . What are you doing here, anyway?"

"I'm going out for a walk," whispered the clerk.

"This is no place for promenading," the policeman retorted angrily. "You've been assigned an apartment and that's where you belong . . . How about it? Don't let me set eyes on you! Riffraff!"

The clerk mumbled something in protest and went home.

"Riffraff, riffraff, riffraff!"

3　　　The policeman paced around his property, searching for offenses. When he entered the yard, thin squeals emanating from the doghouse caught his attention. He was vexed to discover that during the night Amina had given birth to puppies.

He said to himself angrily: "That's all I needed. Can't a person ever have a moment's joy in this world? You miserable hound, who gave you permission to do this? In this house everybody does as they damn well please, as if I wasn't their landlord. One's own bitch gives a man trouble. This must be the tailor's handiwork. I expressly forbade his dog to enter the yard, and this is how my regulations are respected. You just wait, you needlepusher, I'll teach you not to defile my dog."

He reached into the doghouse and pulled out seven multicolored puppies woefully squirming on the ground.

"Shame on you," he said reproachfully to the dog. "Isn't it enough that I have a hard time with my tenants, without you adding to your master's troubles? All right, then."

He took six of the puppies and drowned them in a bucket of rainwater, ignoring Amina, who tried to soothe her maternal agony by silently moaning.

"I'll keep one alive," the policeman mused. "It will grow

up to be a guard dog. And as for you," he turned to the mother, "you'll leave my house if you can't appreciate the good position you have here."

4   It was getting dark when the policeman came home, filled with thoughts of human baseness. His apartment was empty and disorderly.

When his wife appeared, the policeman turned on her angrily: "Where have you been loitering around all this time?"

"Loitering around?" countered his wife. "I was at the grocer's."

The policeman frowned. He recalled the debauched dog, and a vague feeling of jealousy stirred in his innards.

"You. . ." he threatened, "watch out! Why do you hang around the grocery all the time? You should be home taking care of things. You're supposed to work, not waste time. I've been noticing for some time the way you wriggle and giggle in front of the grocer. You slut! If I ever catch you cheating on me, you'll find out who your master is."

And he stuck his fist under his wife's nose.

"You should be ashamed to talk such nonsense," the policeman's wife protested heatedly. "As if I didn't know my place. . ."

"Silence!" the policeman bellowed. "Get out of my sight. You all treat me any way you please, but I'll fix you!"

He turned on the lamp, prepared his writing utensils, and after a little thought began to write. From his hand issued the following document:

Chapter Thirty-one

1   At the beginning of October the terrible event occurred which so agitated the inhabitants of the quarter lying between the two hills.

The clerk came home from the office, but he didn't find any soup on the table. The fire in the oven had gone out; and his wife was not in the kitchen. Worried, the clerk began to look for her and found her in the bedroom; she was convulsed with sobbing.

"Marie," he asked anxiously, "what happened? Why are you crying?"

His wife didn't answer. She continued to weep.

The clerk sat down next to her on the couch.

"Marie," he insisted, "talk to me. Are you sick?"

After some time, his wife began to tell him the story. From her disjointed account, he learned that she had wanted to do the laundry, but found the laundry room locked. When she asked for the key, the usual ugly scene ensued.

"And he insulted me terribly," she sobbed.

"What did he say?"

"He called me names like I was . . . a loose woman . . . He used such a word. . ."

"He called me. . . he called me. . . 'slut'. . ."

The clerk winced.

"He dared to call you that?" he stuttered.

His veins filled with red fury. He felt something giving way inside of him. Red and green dots swirled before his eyes.

Beside himself, he rushed into the yard. There stood the policeman, feeding his rabbits. He fell upon the policeman with the mad courage of a hen attacking a hawk; he tore at his jacket and beat his face with his fists, shouting like a madman.

Surprised, the policeman stepped back. "Huh!" he said in amazement. He was ready to make a move to knock the clerk to the ground. Suddenly, though, an idea flashed through his head: "To raise a hand. . ." He was overjoyed, but covering his face with his hand, he shouted pitifully: "Help me, good people, come and see how Mr. Syrovy treats his landlord. He is trying to kill me and I stand here defenseless. I fear for my very life. You see that I am as mild as a sheep and yet he is using rough force against me."

The clerk came to his senses, and was ashamed.

The policeman said solemnly: "You'll pay for this, Mr. Syrovy. You've committed a serious crime, which is punishable by a long prison term. You have attacked a police officer with murderous intent, and what's more: you have used physical force against your landlord. You'll suffer heavily. I'll make you rot in prison."

The clerk crawled back to his apartment as if in a dream. His legs were stiff as wood and he was shaking feverishly. His wife undressed him and put him to bed.

"This is the end," the clerk whispered and shut his eyes.

2 "Now I'll file my report," the policeman thought to himself. "He'll be bound hand and foot and sent to prison. On the basis of the court decision I'll put in an eviction request."

He spread his arms and said to the invisible court: "Honorable Court, do not be misled by the fact that the accused is a government employee. He is a person dangerous to human life and I cannot allow him to stay in my house. Did he not come close to murdering me?"

And he added silently: "I'll be able to get a down payment of thirty thousand for the apartment. . ."

At that moment he spotted the clerk's father-in-law, who was climbing up the stairs.

After a word of greeting, his father-in-law said: "The summer is gone before we knew it. Now comes autumn, and then winter. That's the ancient order of things."

"That is correct, sir," the policeman answered cheerfully. He thought: "Let him see the difference between a decent person and a criminal."

He continued: "The winds are picking up, and we'll have to get a supply of coal ready for winter. How time passes."

"That's right, my good fellow," said Father. "We are rushing to the grave. Only today I told my wife that I won't be with her much longer. . ."

The policeman was trying to think of something to confirm the old man's good impression of him.

"Shall I give him an aster? Why not," he decided; "it's going to rot anyway."

He went to the garden and snapped off a flower.

"Here, this is for you," he said. "I want everyone to be happy."

Father accepted the flower with thanks and went into the house.

He said to his daughter: "Your landlord is a good man. He gave me this flower. May the Lord give him long life. And where is Jindrich?"

"In bed," whispered his daughter. "He's sick."

"Sick?" he said in alarm. "What is the trouble? I bet it was that evil wind. The weather these days is downright criminal. I'll bring him some medicine; that will make him as good as new."

He launched into a long discourse to the effect that it's bad to be sick and better to be well. Then he left.

3 Drenched by cold perspiration, the clerk kept tossing under the blanket from one side to the other. His wife sat by his side, troubled by unhappy thoughts.

"My life is ruined," the clerk ruminated. "Now they'll come and get me and take me to jail. They'll dismiss me from the office, for no criminal can hold a government job. I'll be humiliated, and my wife, too, will suffer shame."

With great effort, he said to his wife: "Now you'll leave me. . ."

"Why would I leave you?" his wife solaced him.

"You can't live with a criminal," moaned the clerk.

"You're not a criminal," she replied, "you're a hero. You courageously stood up for your wife. Everyone will praise you. . ."

"You know. . ." the clerk whispered secretively, ". . . if they put me in prison, pretend you don't know me . . . I have friends who will help me out of prison. I'll escape abroad and then we'll meet and start a new life. . ."

"He's delirious," Mrs. Syrovy thought. "I'd better call a doctor."

The clerk fell into deep, feverish slumber. His wife tip-toed out of the room in order to call the doctor.

4   A great campfire burns on top of the hill, surrounded by people singing in unison:

> *Down with payments, down with rents —*
> *Alas, alas!*
> *The poor clerk can't sit still,*
> *They made him pay the water bill,*
> *Alas, alas!*

"There seems to be some sort of conspiracy up there," the clerk mumbled and ran up the hill. But he found that the figures around the fire who had sung the song were not people but rabbits. On seeing the clerk, they wrinkled their noses derisively, jumped up, bound the clerk in chains, and led him to the garden. A hen ran ahead of them, shouting: "They've got him, they've got him!" It occurred to the clerk that the hen's name was Anastazie.

They brought him before the policeman, who sat on an overturned wheelbarrow.

The policeman said: "I am Policeman the First and I rule over a fiefdom with an area of six thousand one hundred and twenty square meters. In this realm I have the power of life and death. Whoever resists my will forfeits his head. Take this clerk and throw him in jail. Let him rot there. I have another tenant waiting, a far better one."

The clerk shouted: "I protest!"

Someone's voice answered: "Where is the patient?"

A fairheaded, pink-skinned doctor entered the room, accompanied by a medicinal smell. The clerk awoke and said with a weak smile: "That was something unheard of, rabbits singing. A really strange dream. . ."

"Tra la, tra la. . ." the doctor sang out and briskly rubbed his pudgy hands. "You're not going to get sick on us, old cavalier, are you?"

He examined the patient, tapped his chest, tickled his back with his ears, performing the ritual whereby medicine men since time immemorial have practiced their profession. On completing the examination, he declared that it was nothing to worry about, unless of course complications were to arise. He prescribed some medicaments, a light diet, and calm, for he was one of those doctors who heals his patients by cheerfulness and solace.

Chapter Thirty-two

1   The clerk's illness awoke sympathy in the street. The grocer Mejstrik announced to his wife that he would visit the patient. "If you go, you'll get in trouble," Mrs. Mejstrik warned. "Things can't get any worse," the grocer answered with a frown.

He chatted with the clerk and pitied his fragile state. He also expressed the hope that improvement wasn't far off.

To Mrs. Syrovy he said: "Your husband need have no fear of any legal trouble. There isn't a single person in the whole street who would testify for the policeman. He came to our house and asked us to testify. I told him I didn't want to have anything to do with it. I didn't see anything because I was in the yard fixing the pump. And my wife was at the Dynbyls to collect."

Leaning close to Mrs. Syrovy, he whispered: "The police-man is a scoundrel, remember that. I have long kept it under wraps, but now I've said it. Everything in due time. I like to get along with everybody, but if that isn't possible I can be mean. Just the other day. . . He sends for coffee. I tell him it's impossible; Sunday laws must be observed. He answers that they don't apply to policemen. But I remem-bered that he had caught me once before with that trick. I left the store to get a screwdriver, but in the meantime my foolish wife sold him what he wanted. Whereupon he announced that he would fine me, to teach me to obey the law. Fine, if that's how you want to play it, that's all right with me. I won't stay here long, anyway. What for? My son, a manager, keeps pestering me that he needs his mother to keep house for him. And the louse doesn't want to get married, even though he could have tons of women. But it's time for me to go."

"Come again, Mr. Mejstrik," said Mrs. Syrovy; "my husband enjoyed your visit very much."

"Certainly," answered the grocer on his way out, "why wouldn't I come, when an old geezer like me can make the gentleman feel better. And you, madam, do be careful with him, so that it doesn't take a turn for the worse. There are such cases, people jump around hoppity-skippity and sud-denly it turns into: oh-no, oh-no! Let him get up a good sweat that drives all the poisons out of the body."

With this piece of good advice he departed.

2   In the afternoon the teacher, Soltys, came to visit. He sat down next to the patient's bed and in a mournful voice intoned words of solace.

"The Lord be with you," he began. "The Lord visited you by way of suffering. Ours is not to complain but to joyfully accept God's blows."

"I am very weak," whispered the clerk. He was pleased and encouraged by the sympathy of others, for he saw that he was not as isolated as he had assumed.

"What a kind person," he thought, moved.

"I bring you a happy message," the teacher continued. "Yesterday Grandpa Hynek again appeared to us. We haven't seen him for a long time, and so we had a pleasant chat with him. Our friend predicted that you will soon get well and gain back your strength. So keep up your hope, hope strengthens a person."

"That is so," the clerk mumbled.

"I met the landlord and warned him to be gentler. Let him look out for his advantage, but without engaging in intrigues. 'Have mercy,' I told him, 'on your neighbors, but above all on yourself. For what profits a man to gain the whole world if he lose his own soul?' I tried to use the word of God to turn him to the right path. He rejected me roughly. He said that he was the landlord and knew perfectly well what is what. He was not going to listen to lectures from tenants. I grieved for him, seeing that he was perishing by his own fault. . ."

He kept talking for a while more in flowery language richly interwoven with biblical citations.

Then he left, leaving the patient two oranges and a bouquet of red dahlias.

3   The teacher was followed by the shoemaker, who brought with him a lot of sound and bustle as well as a large, yellowed, dog-eared tome.

"I brought you something to read, Mr. Syrovy," he said. "You'll really enjoy it and the time will pass more quickly. It's an old-fashioned book. I used to carry it around with me when I was a traveling apprentice. I never parted with it and still read it in my spare time. It contains truthful descriptions of the ways of this world . . . A certain scoundrel of a count wanted to deprive his attractive countess of her inheritance. She was an orphan, gentle and quiet. Her name was Angelika. Kuna, the count, hid away the will and unjustly ruled over the realm. With the connivance of the clergy he cast Angelika into a deep dungeon, where the poor girl suffered until she was rescued by Anselm, an honest servant who knew the whole story and had found the will. Angelika later married the knight Rupert, but it took a long time until the wedding took place, and before that she suffered a great deal from that scoundrel Kuna. I would give that swine a good thrashing if I ever got my hands on him . . . This shows that kindheartedness doesn't get you very far and that such types have to be dealt with sternly. They have big eyes and they'd love to gobble up everybody's property, but enough is enough. If people stick together, then all the schemes to rob their pockets are of no use . . . I am a big believer in reading, because a person learns a lot, but it's got to be truthful, like this book. It contains pictures, too, which are very lifelike, especially the one showing Jakub in armor, carrying little Jetrich out of the burning palace. . ."

"Thank you, Mr. Supita," the clerk said warmly.

"It's nothing," the shoemaker replied and then continued: "Remember that I am going to stand up for you. I saw very well how you gave that flatfoot the business. That's the way to do it. It's best to punch such a lout in the stomach, and when he's gasping for breath knock him over the head. That'll make him stop whistling. I have it all worked out, believe me. Many scoundrels still remember the weight of my fist. . ."

"If they take me to prison. . ." began the clerk.

"You won't have to worry," the shoemaker interrupted, "for the best people have languished in dungeons. Like in this novel that I brought you, there was a certain bishop Silvio; they put him in a dark cell, because he refused to swear falsely . . . And as far as the policeman bringing charges against you, remember that I and all the rest of us will swear that we never saw a thing. . ."

The shoemaker's talk pleased the clerk very much . . . Then the patient fell into uneasy slumber.

4   He had a dream: He was standing in a yard full of empty crates. These crates were piled up on top of one another, but in such a way that the smallest was at the bottom, the next biggest on top of that one, and so on until the biggest of all was uppermost. The pile of crates was unsteady and threatened to collapse.

The policeman was standing next to the clerk. He was a small boy in short pants, with a ruff collar around his neck. All the same, the clerk knew that the boy was the policeman. And he wondered: "How come the policeman is wearing that kind of collar?" But he himself was also just a child and wore a sailor cap on his head. The cap bore an inscription in gold letters: "Oh, heart of man, become not the heart of a predator!"

The policeman ordered: "Hold those crates!"

"I won't," countered the clerk. "Hold 'em yourself!"

"If you don't hold them," the policeman threatened, "everything will fall down and there'll be a terrible disaster. Just hold them for a minute, I have to go somewhere. When I come back, I'll take over for you."

The clerk consented and held on to the crates.

The policeman jumped to the side and guffawed: "Now you'll be holding on till the end of the world."

The clerk saw that he'd been deceived, and he wept. The policeman went away, leaving the clerk in a desperate plight.

He stood alongside the pile and held on . . . It was getting dark, and nobody heard his pitiful cries, nobody came to his rescue.

The clerk was about to faint.

"It doesn't matter anymore," he thought in desperation. "I'll let go!"

He closed his eyes and jumped to the side. To his amazement, the pile did not come crashing down. On the contrary, the crates opened and he saw joyfully that they were full of foreign postage stamps. . .

Enormously pleased, he woke up. He felt as though his dejection had vanished, and he said: "Perhaps they won't even send me to prison . . . Perhaps it will all turn out well. . ."

"Certainly," his wife agreed, and prepared to cook the patient two soft-boiled eggs.

Chapter Thirty-three

1   In a few days he had improved to such an extent that he could go back to work. But he was still as feeble as a butterfly in autumn when he stepped out of the house that foggy October day.

At the office his colleagues inquired about the nature and course of his illness with that special kind of interest in medical problems exhibited by clerical workers.

"Yes. . ." an elderly official sighed, "it's that time of year. In nineteen-twenty I felt the hand of death reaching out for me; it was the period when the Spanish flu was at its worst. So I went to the tavern and poured ten shots down my gullet, and that chased the wretched thing away. Believe me, that's the best medicine."

The clerk sat down at his desk to begin his normal work.

A while later the older man spoke up again: "Oh, I almost forgot. You had a phone call yesterday."

The clerk felt his blood turn to jelly.

"Here it is. . .!" he thought with horror. "They're looking for me. I was hoping they'd forget, but they didn't. . ."

"What sort of phone call?" he asked timidly. "What did they want? I don't know anything. . ."

"Wait a moment. . ." answered his colleague, "I have a note somewhere . . . Ah, here it is: A notary named Dr. Werich asked that you stop by his office this morning. . ."

"Who is Dr. Werich?" the clerk protested. "I don't know the man. Let them leave me alone. I'm fresh out of a sickbed. . ."

"Dr. Werich, notary, Platner Street 27," the co-worker repeated, looking at his notebook.

"I don't know anything and I don't want to have anything to do with him," the clerk said heatedly. "I try to stay out of everyone's way, and what do I care about notaries?"

"Maybe it's just a matter of needing some data or something like that. . ." his colleague said soothingly.

"Data. . ." the clerk muttered. "They say data, and suddenly there's some plot behind it. . ."

Nevertheless, after a few minutes of deliberation he got up and left the office, in order to look up the notary. He stopped in front of house No. 27 and pondered: "Perhaps it's nothing urgent. Perhaps I could take care of this later. I have a big backlog of work on my desk, as anyone can see. I can't just waste my time on notaries. . ."

2   Silently protesting, he climbed to the third floor. He stopped in front of the notary's door to catch his breath. His heart pounded in his throat. He pressed the doorbell as gingerly as if he were touching a hot stove. A bell rang out in the hall. The clerk flinched.

"What noise. . .! I'll disrupt the entire house. . ."

A man in a legal secretary's waistcoat opened the door and asked the visitor in. The clerk gave his name, the waistcoat scrutinized him over his glasses and bade him sit down.

"Stare all you like," the clerk muttered to himself resentfully, "I just told you I am Syrovy. I have nothing to hide. . ."

A while later the secretary emerged again and invited Mr. Syrovy to come into his chief's office.

"All right," the clerk sighed and reminded himself to be on his guard.

The notary, a tiny man dry as a willow, with a big head, asked the clerk in a raspy voice: "Mr. Syrovy?"

"That's right," the clerk wheezed with an effort.

The notary cracked his knuckles.

"Ahem . . . do you happen to be a relative of the deceased Mister Krystof Kunstmuller, retired financial counselor?"

The clerk tensed. Deceased Mister Kunstmuller? What sort of trick is this?

"I am his relative," he said; "he is my great-uncle . . . but . . . I know nothing about his death . . . I don't pay attention to such things. . ."

He wiped his forehead with his handkerchief and babbled: "And as far as that affair with my landlord is concerned, please consider . . . I acted out of uncontrollable impulse . . . I beg you not to believe gossip. . ."

The notary looked severely at Mr. Syrovy.

"That is beside the point," he said. "Ahem . . . let's continue. In his last will, Mr. Kunstmuller named you his sole heir and empowered me to execute his testament."

The clerk shivered.

The notary continued, looking at the documents laid out on the desk: "The inheritance consists of a house in the Avenue of the Resistance, Number 23. . ." (one finger), and of liquid assets . . . let's see . . . that comes to eight hundred thirty-five thousand crowns (a second finger)."

It suddenly seemed to the clerk that the walls parted and the notary's armchair went flying out of the room. Windows and doors turned into a kind of foggy liquid; the din of a waterfall resounded from somewhere. Red and violet wheels sailed majestically into the room and danced gravely around the chandelier.

At last the clerk came to his senses.

"Sorry, don't mind me. . ." he excused himself hurriedly. "I'm a little feeble . . . after my sickness. Excuse me."

The notary nodded.

"So there we have it," he said. He buttoned his jacket and stood up.

"It's up to you to claim the inheritance, which is of course just a formality, and to pay the inheritance tax." He shook the clerk's hand.

"Sir," Mr. Syrovy mumbled humbly, "I am ready . . . to do everything."

He suddenly broke into tears.

"Please, don't do me an injustice. . ." he sobbed. "Everybody will give you the best reports about me . . . everything happened against my will. . ."

The notary was frightened.

"What's that?" he exclaimed. "What kind of talk is this?"

Everything became confused. The clerk seemed out of his mind; he saw nothing, he heard nothing. He was only aware that the waistcoated secretary led him down the stairs and remonstrated with him in an earnest voice.

3   Somehow or other the clerk found himself in the street.

"Everything inside me congealed."

This sentence, spoken aloud, woke the clerk out of his strange paralysis. The stream of pedestrians pushed him aside into one of the old-town passageways. He shook like a puppy and spoke confused words.

"Certainly. . . certainly. . . I had fallen into error," he reassured himself, gesturing with his hands. "I must initiate. . . initiate what? Wait!" he reminded himself sharply. "First I must think it out. I know everything, gentlemen . . . you want me to pay inheritance taxes? Oh, mister notary!" he called out with bitter irony. "That isn't nice of you, my dear sir . . . With your permission I'd like to ask you something. You speak of liquid assets — real estate, transference charges . . . please express yourself plainly . . . what's your game? I know who my friends are and who wishes me ill. . ."

He waved his arm and added mournfully: "It's a lot of nonsense anyway."

Suddenly his head lit up as if he had a short-circuit in his brain. He caught his breath.

"But actually," he exclaimed in amazement, "actually I am rich! It's a revolution, a real hurricane! Rejoice, friend, your troubles are over!"

He rushed out of the passageway like a madman and galloped down the street. He laughed crazily and told himself: "Slow down, slow down, friend, it seems you're getting out of hand. . ."

He didn't see, he didn't hear, he was wild as a grouse at harvest time. He jostled a woman. She shouted: "Can't you look where you're going, you fool? Shame on you! It's the middle of the day and he's as drunk as a sailor. You should be ashamed, a young fellow like you!"

"Madam," the clerk excused himself, "I didn't mean to hurt you. And I am not at all drunk. I have never been drunk, except the night of graduation when we celebrated a bit. But that was excusable on account of my youth. You would have to understand the circumstances. So please don't scold me any further, I won't allow. . ."

He turned to the crowd which had gathered around him.

"Gentlemen," he said, "be my witnesses that I meant no harm. . ."

The woman spat and left.

The clerk continued on his way.

He babbled: "Now I'll cultivate miniature hyacinths, for

real . . . one row of gentian, then tulips . . . and perennials, you'll see such perennials. . .!"

He stopped himself short; an ugly thought clutched at his throat.

"What am I celebrating about? What am I doing? I'm a fool! The word of some notary. . .? Maybe it's all a swindle . . . Do I ever have any luck? I believe anything people tell me . . ."

4   And he recalled a dream he'd had as a child.

He used to attend kindergarten at a convent. At Christmas time, the nuns gave the children presents. Jindrich's present was different from all the others; it was just an empty yeast box, but it had magical powers. When he sat down on it, it flew through the air, not violently or high, but just slightly off the ground, sailing down the street with a graceful, gentle motion. He was overjoyed and said: "I'll fly to our house and show Mom and Dad this wonderful box."

He flew to the front of the house and called his parents to show off his gift. His parents came out and Jindrich sat down on the box. But the box didn't budge, no matter how he tried. Everyone laughed at him.

The clerk thought morosely: "And so everything was spoiled. That's just my kind of luck. I don't recall that a pretty girl ever sat down next to me on the streetcar . . . But I'm not going to let that notary get away with making fun of me . . . I'll show him. . .!"

He rushed to Platner Street and all out of breath climbed to the third floor. He stopped in front of the notary's door.

"Shall I ring the bell . . . or not?" he hesitated.

Then his eye caught a sign

| HANNA ROUBICKOVA |
| modes-robes |

"If that sign contains an odd number of letters," he decided, "then I'll ring; if it's even — then I won't."

The sign contained an odd number of letters.

"Shall I ring then? But perhaps I should have counted the hyphen between modes and robes?"

At that moment the door opened, and the notary stepped out to check his mailbox. On seeing the clerk, he was somewhat startled, and then asked in a kindly tone: "Did you forget something?"

"No, no," the clerk assured him hastily, "I only. . ."

He bowed and left.

He suddenly realized that it was all true.

Chapter Thirty-four

1   He felt unusually strong and fresh. The sun broke through the fog and filled the streets with gentle warmth.

"My sun of glory has risen," the clerk thought loftily; but he immediately pulled himself up. "Slowly, slowly; no bombast. We're an adult."

He walked along at a good pace, his head held high. People rushed by him. With proud self-awareness he pitied them for having to scrape around for a livelihood. In the window of a gourmet shop he saw the figure of a Chinaman who was recommending a certain brand of tea. He stopped and examined him with amusement. Then he blew him a kiss.

"I could buy that Chinaman if I wanted to," he told himself, "but I don't. I'll buy myself an ivory chess set and a Peugeot car. That's my favorite make of car."

It seemed to him that he had grown three heads taller. He was very surprised when he saw his reflection in the mirror of a furniture store; his figure was negligible, he had a hunched back and a birdlike face, just as before the revolution.

"The mirror is deceptive," he said to himself with confidence.

For he felt himself growing and his shoulders broadening. Before he reached his house he was mighty as an imperial guard. From a distance he saw the policeman's house; it was tiny as a box of matches. As if he were looking at it through the wrong end of a telescope, that's how insignificant it was.

"Should I knock him to the ground?" the clerk asked himself. "Why shouldn't I? I could crush him between my fingers like a dead bed-bug. Let him rescue himself before I arrive; because I'll crush him, I'll crush him to bits."

But the closer he came to the house, the bigger the policeman grew. And the clerk was gradually shrinking.

The policeman grew and grew, wider and mightier, until he was one hundred and seventy five yards tall, one hundred seventy five yards wide. His head loomed over the hill; his shadow covered the entire street. And the clerk turned into a tiny insect, invisible to the naked eye.

Passing the policeman, he involuntarily reached up and doffed his hat. The surprised policeman touched his cap and muttered something. For a few moments he kept watching the door behind which his tenant had disappeared, and then he said victoriously: "I taught them some manners."

2   "Is this any time to come home?"

The clerk remained gloomily silent.

"Is three-thirty any time to come home for dinner?" repeated Mrs. Syrovy. And she showered the clerk with a stream of reproaches. Nobody can expect her to stand guard over the stove. She hasn't got time for such nonsense. But he has no consideration. He forgets that his wife has to wash dishes and clean the house. Let him see for himself what the kitchen looks like. If anybody came in and saw that mess, she would die of shame.

The clerk humbly bent his head over the soup plate, picked up a bit of salt on the tip of his knife, and grumbled: "Another sermon . . . I wonder if this goes on in other households. Go and see him yourself . . . let them leave me alone with their summonses."

His wife was puzzled: "Where should I go?"

"To him . . . To the notary. . ." answered the clerk.

"And what would I do at the notary's?"

"Of course it's all right for me to chase after notaries," the clerk complained. "Everything's up to me, I've got to worry about everything . . . He talks to me about inheritance taxes, and makes me late for dinner. I don't need his lectures; I know what it's all about . . . So as you see, it's not my fault that I got held up. . ."

Mrs. Syrovy was startled. "What notary are you talking about and what did you do there?"

The clerk got angry and quarrelsome. Along with reproaches he spoke confusedly about inheritance, liquid assets, real estate, rents, and money.

His wife looked him sharply in the face and said: "You see, I told you to put on that knitted vest when you go to the office. As soon as you finish eating you'll go to bed . . . That's what happens when people don't listen."

She put the clerk to bed and began cleaning the house.

But the words about an inheritance stuck in her head. Something resembling a tiny hope germinated in her breast.

What if. . .?

Stubbornly she kept resisting the idea, for all thoughts of happiness seem to the oppressed like a frivolous challenge to fate.

Nevertheless, she asked the clerk, off-hand and with an indifferent face, for the notary's address. And then she slipped out of the house.

In the evening she returned, a radiant, beautiful woman. Her face was flushed and the wrinkles around her eyes, etched by time and worry, had disappeared. She brought the clerk a bunch of blue grapes.

"Here you are, dear," she said tenderly; "eat and you'll be refreshed."

"So you see that I was right," answered the clerk, picking off the grapes with satisfaction. He calmed down and regained his poise when he saw that his wife believed him.

3   Eagerly, they began to discuss the future. In her imagination, the wife marched triumphantly into their new household at the head of an army of women armed with wet rags, brooms, and brushes. She turned everything upside down, administered alterations, positioned the furniture.

"And I'll hire a maid," she said.

"Naturally," the clerk agreed.

He grew animated, jumped out of bed, and started pacing the room.

"What a revolution, what a change!" he raved. "It's the end of misery, new horizons have opened up . . . It's hard to believe!"

He paused and looked sternly at his wife. A tiny hint of suspicion hissed once more in his mind.

"I hope," he said, "that you didn't let yourself be fooled and that everything is in order. . ."

"Of course," his wife answered.

Her calm tone satisfied the clerk. Once again, he grew animated: "A glorious life beckons . . . Of course, we will not surrender to luxury; rather, we will live decently and in accord with our position. . ."

His wife woke from her musings.

"Too bad," she sighed.

"What's too bad?" the clerk asked.

"Eight hundred and thirty-five thousand . . . Too bad it's not a whole million . . ."

"Why?"

"I don't know . . . A million would be such an even number. . ."

"Marie, don't blaspheme," the clerk said gravely; "eight hundred and thirty-five thousand is quite a pretty sum."

"That's not the point. It simply seems strange to me that if he could manage to save eight hundred and thirty-five thousand, he didn't save up an even million."

"Don't tarnish my uncle's memory. He was a scholar and a kind-hearted person. You ought to thank the Lord that you picked me as your husband, a person blessed with such excellent relatives."

"I've lived with you in hard times, and I'll know how to live in wealth, too."

"That's right . . . And I'll be an entirely different kind of landlord than our policeman, you'll see. In my house the tenants will live in peace and quiet . . . Of course, the outside doors of the tenants' apartments will be painted brown, whereas my door will have the look of sparkling enamel . . . And in front of the door there will be a mat with the inscription 'Hail.' For it is fitting for a landlord to distinguish himself in the eyes of the tenants. . ."

"I'll buy you material for suits," said his wife, "so that you'll be dressed as befits your status."

"But I'll have to come along. I can't allow you to pick another eccentric design."

"That was a different matter," his wife tried to justify herself, "the material was firm and lasting. You got lots of use out of that suit. Now, of course, you can afford something more elegant."

She thought for a moment. Then she said: "We will have to give him notice."

"Without a doubt," the clerk said self-confidently. "I'll have a talk with him."

"That won't be necessary. We'll send him a written notice."

"You're right. That's even better."

They kept talking a while longer and then they stepped out for some air. They felt their apartment too confining.

It occurred to the wife to visit her parents in order to inform them of the great news. They went to town.

Father was sitting on the couch, smoking his meerschaum and gazing pensively at the star on the ceiling. He was in the midst of recounting some sort of story to his wife:

". . . so I said to him: 'Innkeeper, you have some strange customs here.' 'What customs?' he says. 'What customs? This one: you serve a decent piece of meat, but only two small potatoes. What's the meaning of that? I am used to a solid portion of potatoes. You won't please me half as much with meat as with potatoes. From my childhood on I've been a potato lover.' He didn't say a thing, just went to the kitchen — and in a minute the waiter brought me a heaping plate of potatoes. You should have seen it. . ."

224

"But did you have to pay extra for the potatoes?" countered his wife.

"Not on your life! I ordered two beers and a cigar, and the whole thing came to seventy-five kreuzer. In those days we still had some old-fashioned Czech values, we didn't have the kind of thievery you see today . . . In that same town I once got into a fight over an ounce of poppy seeds. . ."

The news of the inheritance created a panic. It was unheard of that a piece of luck, such as winning the lottery or inheriting money, would ever happen to the poor. Such events happened only in fairy tales. Mother came unstrung and kept running aimlessly back and forth. Half-consciously, led by a powerful habit, she made coffee. In his enthusiasm, Father emitted sounds similar to those of a creaky couch.

Mother cried and embraced her daughter. Father declared that it was necessary to take everything firmly in hand. A person had certain obligations toward property.

They stayed up long into the night, discussing the pleasurable life that was in the offing.

Chapter Thirty-five

1   "... as of the next quarter, namely the first of the year, I hereby give notice of moving out..."

Again and again the policeman kept returning to that sentence, which confused him no end.

"What's that?" he pondered, pacing the room with long steps. "Why are they giving me notice? It happened so suddenly, I can't understand it."

Maybe the clerk had become frightened of criminal charges connected with the violence ... He thought about it, but then decided that was not the reason. The clerk surely knew that the neighbors had refused to testify in the case. And these days not even the word of a policeman is trusted in court.

"Maybe they suddenly came into some money..."

That was possible, though it seemed strange. Besides, where would anyone find an apartment that quickly these days? They seem to be under the impression that other landlords would jump for joy at their coming, but they are very mistaken, I can guarantee it. Maybe they think I'll break down and cry. Oh no, my friends! I can get a dozen better than they.

The policeman felt that he ought to be pleased, because he had succeeded in accomplishing what he had so long been hoping for.

"I am pleased, mighty pleased," he thought to himself, "that I can make a nice little profit on that apartment. The house is built and I can ask for higher rents. You helped me to do that, ha ha...!"

Nevertheless, he felt no pleasure. On the contrary, confusion was growing inside of him and he was caught in a web of doubts.

"Did I perhaps miscalculate, pressing them so hard? What the devil! Good riddance, I won't be calling you back. You've caused me enough trouble already. . ."

What trouble? Actually, they weren't all that bad. There are worse tenants.

"He was tolerable. I could put up with him. But she's a pest!"

Anyway, why worry? Mustn't listen to a lot of gossip. And yet, did he do something wrong to cause such a turn-about?

"Damn it!" he cursed aloud. "I have to look into it!"

He put on his cap and set out toward the house.

On the street he ran into his wife. She was so excited her eyes were popping out of her head.

"What is it?" the policeman asked. "Where were you?"

"In the laundry room . . . They told me everything. . ."

"What did they tell you?"

"You pound your beat all day and yet know nothing . . . They inherited. . . They inherited a house plus thousands!"

"Who? Who inherited?"

"Who, who," hooted his wife. "The Syrovys inherited a house plus thousands . . . what am I saying: Millions! Millions, can you imagine? I have it first-hand. . ."

The policeman was thunderstruck.

"So that's how it is!" he disburdened himself.

Overcoming his surprise, he felt his anger rising.

"You. . ." he shouted, and waived his fist at his wife. "Instead of sitting at home, you chase after gossip. You kept annoying them until you hounded them out of the house. I'll fix you this evening. . .!" And he rushed off, panting with anger.

2   He found the clerk out on the terrace; he was sitting in a chair, reading the paper with the calm expression of a man who is set for life.

The policeman felt a surge of fury. "He's ignoring the rules!" flashed through his mind. But realizing that he was now dealing with a person who had freed himself from subservience, he controlled himself, and the troubled surface of his petty-officer soul calmed down. He greeted the clerk.

The clerk shuddered.

"Resting after work?" the policeman asked amicably. "That's good, that's good . . . The office is probably stuffy, and it's pleasant to sit in the fresh air. A bit of rest and back to work, that's the best way. . ."

The clerk perked up and agreed that rest after work is pleasant.

"By the way. . ." the policeman said, "how come you want to leave us? Don't you like my house anymore? True, we had some misunderstandings, but I have figured it all out. I can now see clearly who was the cause of all the trouble. I'll issue an order that. . . Everything will be all right. I'll make you the chief over the other tenants and your word will count as much as mine. . ."

The clerk answered to the effect that unfortunately he wouldn't be able to take advantage of the landlord's kindly regulations and reform efforts. In a short time he intends to move to a place of his own.

The policeman sadly nodded his head.

"And here I thought," he sighed with deep emotion, "that we would never part, that we would remain true to one another . . . So you are moving to your own place? That's fine, I congratulate you . . . Now it stands this way: I am an owner and you are an owner. We're both of us owners, ha ha . . . only you're a big owner and I'm a small one. . ."

The policeman kept chattering away; words flowed from his lips like syrup. His talk was beginning to make the clerk nauseous. He got up, ready to leave.

The policeman stepped up to him and, breathing intimately into his face, he said: "But I have one piece of advice for you, Mr. Syrovy, for your new life . . . You have to be strict with your tenants, because tenants are a miserable lot. I have plenty of experience. I'm telling you as an experienced owner. We owners must stick together. . ."

"Jindrich!" Mrs. Syrovy called from the house.

"Madame Syrovy is calling," the policeman pointed out; "perhaps she has prepared some refreshments for you after your work at the office. That's how it ought to be. I approve."

The clerk left. The policeman said to himself: "A big owner, and yet he was quite friendly toward me, a little owner."

3 "Madam," the grocer said to Mrs. Syrovy, "good luck just had to come your way, because you are so sincere with everyone. The Good Lord cleverly arranged for you to be heirs. Everybody gets what they deserve. He couldn't watch your troubles any longer, and so He made everything turn out all right. Everything in this world is by design: If you're fated to hang, you won't drown. That scoundrel of a policeman plays tricks on everyone, but you just wait! Everything in due time."

"Mejstrik!" his wife cautioned. "Watch your tongue!"

"I've been careful a long time, Majdalena," the grocer replied, "and it hasn't done me a bit of good. He plotted against us anyway, and caused trouble whenever he could. Now we're selling our business, and so we can afford to have personal opinions. As long as a man is running a business, he has to reign himself in. What is Mr. Supita bringing us?"

The shoemaker reached out his hand, black with cobbler's glue, to Mrs. Syrovy and declaimed: "Three cheers and a hurrah! The day of liberation from the bonds of the oppressor dawns . . . Down with police tyranny! Long live the humble citizenry!"

He winked at the grocer and said: "I've been bending the elbow a bit, out of sheer joy. May I be forgiven. I haven't had a drink since the cobblers' ball. I'll fix that flatfoot, if I have to go to jail for it. And besides, I'm going to send an item to the newspaper; I have it all lined up in my head. I'll write up his whole life history and his goings on, so the public can see the kind of specimen we're dealing with . . . Yes, definitely. . ."

And he burst into a mighty song. Mrs. Supita came running in and with loud admonishments led her husband away.

4   The policeman was dabbling in the garden, immersed in thoughts of money and unexpected windfalls.

He thought: "One man must sweat out every penny, and another just has money fall in his lap. Explain it if you can. . ."

He frowned; envy was eating him up. He glanced at the house and saw the news dealer's wife standing in the door; he noticed that her hips had grown wider.

He stepped up to her and said: "What is this I see? How dare you . . . Children aren't part of our deal. . ."

"But. . ." the woman protested.

"Quiet! No buts! Everyone around here seems to be doing whatever they please. I took you in as a childless couple. There isn't a word about children in our contract.

Children lower the value of real estate. People will say: 'Mr. Faktor's house is full of a bunch of brats' and I won't get a decent tenant. Anyway, I've noticed that you've been thumbing your nose at me. I ordered you to keep my mother's grave in good shape; recently I went to the cemetery and I saw a mess . . . Is that supposed to be a grave? That's a pile of manure, not a grave. Makes me ashamed before the world. It looks like I'll have to get tough with you . . . You were supposed to fill the lamp with oil. Have you been doing it?"

"I have. . ." gulped the news dealer's wife.

"You haven't! The lamp was out. I'll have to keep my eye on you. You instigated against the Syrovys and now they're leaving me. You wander all over the neighborhood even though I ordered the tenants to stay in their apartments. You'll pay for it! I'll show you. . ."

After the woman left, he clenched his fists and fumed: "Two-bit tenants! There's no profit in them, and they do as they please. The news dealer's got to go. I keep on paying interest, like throwing my money into a bottomless pit. And they have no appreciation. Oh, nobody would believe what scum I have in my house. . ."

Chapter Thirty-six

1   A few months passed, and the hills were covered with snow. Frosty wind blew through the streets and people said: "Oh my, this really chills your bones!" Children with sleds clambered up the slopes.

The Syrovys made preparations for moving. Mrs. Syrovy was packing, and her husband, who had resolved to be useful, kept stumbling among the scattered objects.

The policeman paced around his house, watched the commotion, and said melancholically: "Well well, so here we are!" Burdened by a secret thought, he kept watch, waiting for the clerk. When Mr. Syrovy stepped out the door, he stopped him and said: "You're really moving?"

"The time has come," answered the clerk.

"How quickly time passes!" said the policeman.

"It makes the mind boggle."

"We hardly met and it's time to part," the policeman said sadly.

"It can't be helped," retorted the clerk.

"A person should never get attached to another person," the policeman philosophized.

"One leaves, another comes," said the clerk.

"It happens so fast," said the policeman.

"It's all a matter of habit," said the clerk.

"We met, we got to know each other, and now it's over."

"You'll get other tenants."

"Only death should break the bonds between tenant and landlord. Otherwise the whole thing is meaningless."

"Too bad it doesn't always work out that way. Life means change."

"That's how it is."

A struggle broke out in the policeman's breast; then he stepped closer to the clerk and said in a muffled voice: "Since we're both owners, just between us . . . I have all sorts of problems now. You can imagine, that's how it goes. We two have always understood one another. I am supposed to give the city five thousand for a sidewalk in front of the house. And the bank originally promised. . . They said to wait until after Christmas, they didn't have the time now . . . And so I thought that you, as a fellow owner. . ."

He kept on talking in the same vein before the clerk realized that the policeman was asking him for a loan. He was seized by a peculiar feeling. He felt ashamed without knowing why; he felt as if he was being forced to eat an unpleasant dish.

At that point Mrs. Syrovy appeared in the door. She said sharply: "Forget it, Mr. Faktor! Why, for heavens' sake, should we lend you money? Didn't you cause us enough unpleasantness? Talk to somebody else, we don't want to know anything about you! Jindrich, come on, let's go home!"

The policeman was taken aback; in a moment, however, he regained his old arrogance.

"All right, you needn't worry," he exclaimed disdainfully, "I wasn't talking to you, my woman. Mr. Syrovy's another matter. I'd be glad to talk with him at midnight, if need be. Five thousand isn't going to make me or break me. It's just possible I have more than you. I've been an owner for a long time, whereas you don't even know what ownership's all about. I'm glad to be getting rid of you; you bring me no profit anyway. And stop hanging around the terrace. You'll obey my regulations as long as you live here. I am still the master here."

2   A few days later, a gentleman appeared in the house on the outskirts of the city. He was dressed in a chauffeur's coat and his huge skull bore a leather cap. He had high cheekbones, a black mustache, and black whiskers. He seemed to have a sign on his forehead that read, "I've been around, you won't get the better of me!"

Chomping on a cigar, he visited the Syrovy apartment, accompanied by the policeman. He examined everything thoroughly, tested with a knowing mien whether the windows and doors closed tight, stuck his head in the oven, and flushed the toilet several times. He did all this with a skeptical look on his face. Then they went out in the yard and the clerk overheard their conversation.

"In my house, Mr. Baloun," said the policeman "you'll live as if in paradise. That's just the kind of person I am. You won't find another landlord like me. Regard for one another, that's my philosophy. I've had a lot of tenants coming to see me, but in vain. I am a careful sort of person. . ."

The man in the chauffeur's uniform shifted his cigar from one corner of his mouth to the other and wheezed: "Sure, sure, that's just a lot of talk. Will there be room for hanging out laundry?"

"You bet!" the policeman declared enthusiastically. "There'll be plenty of room! I'll fix up everything the way you want it. The main thing is mutual trust. Right here, in front of the house, there will be a basin with a fountain. Perhaps I'll even put in some goldfish."

"I don't care about the goldfish," said the man, "but I want to know if the cellar can be locked. If anybody were

234

to filch my coal, I'd break his leg in two; I'm a choleric type."

"You needn't concern yourself," the policeman said earnestly. "I love order myself. I see that we are beginning to understand each other. As soon as I first laid eyes on you, I said to myself that we won't part, we'll stick together."

"That's no problem," said Mr. Baloun. "I'm all for that. Give and take. I'm not a tightwad, but I won't let myself be cheated. I'll pay and I want what's coming to me. I won't budge from that."

"Exactly how I feel!" enthused the policeman. "Oh, I know you'll be happy here with us. Look, right here, where we're standing, I'll plant a linden tree. It will grow into a real honest Slavic linden, you know. And under that linden we'll sit together in harmony. . ."

"Well. . ." the fellow in the chauffeur's coat muttered, "a linden . . . What good is a tree like that? The main thing is: where can I attach my antenna? I like music, and if can't play my radio then forget the whole thing."

"Of course," answered the policeman, "of course, Mr. Baloun. You'll have your radio, you'll have everything. All your wishes will be taken care of, I'll see to that. . ."

They kept on chatting in this vein and then the policeman accompanied the new tenant to the gate.

3 Toward the end of the year, the Syrovys moved out. The van arrived and the movers began to load the furniture. The street gathered and expressed its sentiments. Acquaintances came to say goodbye. The grocer stepped out the door and waved. The shoemaker came running, his bare feet shod in slippers, and hailed the Syrovys.

The teacher, Mr. Soltys, shook the clerk's hand and said

melancholically: "You're leaving, but we remain in Babylonian captivity."

"Your day of liberation will arrive," the clerk answered.

The teacher shook his head. He said quietly: "Grandpa Hynek is of the opinion that we must drink the bitter cup to the bottom. For you, though, he predicts happy and contented times."

"Your Grandpa Hynek is a good, wise man," the clerk answered, much moved. "The next time you talk to him, please give him my respects."

"Thank you, I will," the teacher said with a bow. "I'll be thinking of you. . ."

Just as the coachman snapped his whip to start the van moving, a limousine pulled up in front of the house. With dignity, Mr. and Mrs. Syrovy stepped in, the chauffeur closed the doors, and the car drove smoothly off.

The clerk looked back. The zig-zag battlements of the house on the outskirts of the city got smaller and smaller. As they turned a corner, the house disappeared from sight.

Epilogue

One beautiful, sunny day, the lawyer with the cold eyes and his bald-headed colleague ran into each other in front of the courthouse.

"Greetings!" said the cold-eyed lawyer. "Where are you off to, honorable colleague?"

"A new case. . ." answered the bald-headed man. "A client of mine is suing his landlord in connection with some sort of linden tree. . ."

"How about that!" the lawyer with the cold eyes exclaimed. "You must represent Mr. Baloun!"

"How did you know?"

"Very simple. I am defending Mr. Faktor."

"Ha, ha! That's a good one! Once again we are on opposite sides!"

"But this time you'll lose, dear colleague. We are under no obligation to provide a linden."

"You are wrong, my good colleague. That linden tree was specified in the contract; it was expressly promised and we insist on it."

"The tree is not part of the contract. It would have been considered a gift, but in that event it would have had to be promised in the presence of a notary."

"What do you mean, gift? Immovable property can be an object of a tenant's contract; in this case, a tree. We shall present witnesses to the effect that my client searched for an apartment where he could live in a spirit of harmony. Mr. Faktor promised to plant a linden tree under which he would sit with my client in harmony. We shall insist on that, even if execution *ad factum praestandum*. . . Anyway, we'll discuss it further before the session. What is your policeman doing these days?"

"What is he doing? People with briefcases are running all over his property."

"Oh! That's bad sign!"

"I figure he won't be able to keep the house. But he's got to have his lawsuits; he goes to court at the drop of a hat, the stubborn fool. . ."

"And my client, his landlady, is the same . . . She's on her way to the poorhouse. Her last house was sold at auction."

The bald-headed lawyer looked at his watch.

"Shall we go? It's time."

The two lawyers disappeared into the courthouse.

Karel Poláček (1892-1944) was one of the leading Czech novelists, journalists, children's writers, and humorists between the wars. He was also the most prominent Jewish author writing in Czech. Like his friend Karel Čapek, he always brought humor and the unexpected to all of his pursuits, and he managed to be a great stylist whose work was, and still is, accessible. Ring Lardner is the English-language writer closest in spirit and style to Poláček. *What Ownership's All About* is the first of Poláček's works to appear in English.

Peter Kussi has translated three of Milan Kundera's novels, including *Immortality*. He has also translated works by such Czech authors as Josef Škvorecký, Jaroslav Hašek, and Jiří Gruša. He teaches at Columbia University.